ELLIOTT'S NEW FRIEND

Michael was on his way out to play football, when his little brother stopped him. "Remember the goblin? I'm gonna show him to you," Elliott said, "but he belongs to me."

"Okay, okay, but make it fast. What is it, a skunk or something? Do you have it in your room? Mom'll kill you."

Elliott led Michael down the hall. "Take off your shoulder pads," he said as they entered the room. "You might scare him."

"Don't push it, Elliott."

Elliott led him to the closet door. "Close your eyes."

"Why?"

"Just do it, Michael . . . "

A STEVEN SPIELBERG FILM

E.T.

THE EXTRA-TERRESTRIAL

A STEVEN SPIELBERG FILM
E.T. THE EXTRA-TERRESTRIAL
DEE WALLACE   PETER COYOTE   DREW BARRYMORE
HENRY THOMAS AS ELLIOTT
MUSIC BY JOHN WILLIAMS
WRITTEN BY MELISSA MATHISON
PRODUCTION DESIGNER JAMES D. BISSELL
DIRECTOR OF PHOTOGRAPHY ALLEN DAVIAU
EDITED BY CAROL LITTLETON
PRODUCED BY STEVEN SPIELBERG & KATHLEEN KENNEDY
DIRECTED BY STEVEN SPIELBERG   A UNIVERSAL RELEASE

Original Soundtrack on MCA Records and Tapes

Other books by William Kotzwinkle

E.T.

THE EXTRA-TERRESTRIAL
in his adventure on earth

a novel by
WILLIAM KOTZWINKLE
based on a screenplay by
MELISSA MATHISON

BERKLEY BOOKS, NEW YORK

E.T.
THE EXTRA-TERRESTRIAL
in his adventure on earth

A Berkley Book / published by arrangement with
MCA Publishing Rights, a Division of MCA INC.

PRINTING HISTORY
Berkley edition / June 1982

A BERKLEY BOOK ® TM 757,375
Berkley Books are published by The Berkley Publishing Group,
200 Madison Avenue, New York, New York 10016.
The name "BERKLEY" and the "B" logo
are trademarks belonging to Berkley Publishing Corporation.
PRINTED IN THE UNITED STATES OF AMERICA

30 29 28 27

E.T.

THE EXTRA-TERRESTRIAL
in his adventure on earth

The spaceship floated gently, anchored by a beam of lavender light to the earth below. Were someone to come upon this landing site, they might, for a moment, think that a gigantic old Christmas tree ornament had fallen from the night sky—for the Ship was round, reflective, and inscribed with a delicate gothic design.

Its mellow radiance, the scattering of something like diamond dust on its hull, would make one look again for the ornamental hook at its point, by which it had hung in a far-off galaxy. But there was no one nearby, and the Ship had landed purposefully, the intelligence commanding it beyond navigational error. Yet an error was about to be made...

The hatch was open, the crew out and about, probing the earth with strangely shaped tools, like little old elves caring for their misty, moonlit gardens. When here and there the mist parted and the pastel light from the Ship's hull fell upon them, it was clear they weren't elves, but creatures more scientifically minded, for they were taking samples—of flowers, moss, shrubs, saplings. Yet their misshapen heads, their drooping arms and roly-poly, sawed-off torsos would make one think of elfland, and the tenderness they showed the plants might add to this impression— were someone of Earth nearby to observe it, but no one was, and the elfin botanists from space were free to work in peace.

Even so, they started in fear when a bat twittered by, or an owl hooted, or a dog barked in the distance. Then their breathing quickened and a mistlike camouflage surrounded them, flowing from their fingertips and from their long toes; then they would be hard indeed to discover; then a solitary walker in the moonlight might pass by the misty patch, never knowing a crew from ancient space huddled there.

The spaceship was another matter. Enormous Victorian Christmas tree ornaments don't fall to the earth with great frequency. Their presence is felt—by radar, by military intuition, by other scanning devices—and this gigantic bauble had been detected. It was too big to be missed; no protective fog could completely cover it, on earth, or swinging in the tree of night. So—an encounter is at hand. Government vehicles are out, government specialists are earning their night's pay, bouncing around the back roads, talking to each other on radios, closing in on the great ornament.

However, the little old crew of botanists are not really disturbed—not yet, in any case. They know they have time; they know, to within the most sub-divided increments of time, how long it will be before the gruff, clumsy noises of earthly vehicles sound in their ears. They have been here before, for the earth is large and there are many plants to pick, if one wishes to have a complete collection.

They continued their sampling, mist flowing about each of them as he walked back with his prize from Earth's soil.

Up the hatchway they went, and into the lovely ornament's interior pastel glow. They moved uncon-cernedly through its pulsing corridors of technological wonders, and into the central wonder of the Ship: a gigantic inner cathedral of Earth's foliage. This im-mense greenhouse was the core of the Ship, its pur-pose, its specialty. Here were lotus flowers from a Hindu lagoon, ferns from the floor of Africa, tiny berries from Tibet, blackberry bushes from a back-country American road. Here, in fact, was one of everything on Earth, or nearly everything—for the job was not yet done.

Everything flourished. Were an expert from one of Earth's great botanical gardens to come into this greenhouse, he would find plants he'd never seen before—except in fossil form, imprinted in coal. His eyes would certainly pop, to find, alive, plants the dinosaurs had dined on, plants from Earth's first gardens incalculable ages ago. He would faint, and be revived with herbs from the Hanging Gardens of Babylon.

From the fanning roofline, moisture dripped, with nutrients that nourished the countless species that embellished every surface of the Ship's core, the most perfect collection of vegetation on Earth, old as the Earth is old, old as the little botanists themselves, who come and go; and the crinkling lines at the corners of their eyes have the look of fossils too, etched over immense ages of gathering.

One of them entered now, carrying a local herb, its leaves already drooping. He took it to a basin and placed it in a liquid that affected its disposition at once, leaves suddenly reviving, roots waving. At the same moment, from a rosette window above the basin, a pastel light came on, bathing the plant and causing it to stand up straight again beside its neighbor, a little flower of antediluvian make.

The extraterrestrial botanist gazed at it for a moment, to see that all was well, then turned and recrossed the greenhouse. He moved beneath Japanese cherry blossoms, hanging Amazon flowers, and some ordinary horseradish that leaned his way lovingly. He patted it and walked on, back through the pulsating corridor and down the glowing hatchway.

Out in the night air, his body exhaled faint mist again, which surrounded him as he walked along to gather more plants. A colleague passed him, holding a wild parsnip root. Their eyes did not meet, but something else took place: their chests glowed simultaneously, an inner red glow from the heart region suffusing their thin, translucent skin. Then they passed, the one with his parsnip and the other, empty-handed, down a rocky incline, his heart-light dark once more. Mist-shrouded, he entered tall grass, tall as his own head, and came out the other side, at the edge of a redwood forest. There, dwarfed by the enormous trees, he turned back toward his Ship, and his heart-light glowed again, as if he were signing to the Ship itself, to the beloved old ornament he'd been riding in for ages. On its catwalks, in its hatchway, other heart-lights glowed, like fireflies moving here and there. Satisfied that his protection was near, and knowing there was still time to work before danger came, he entered the redwood forest.

Nighthawks sang, insects creaked in the shadows, and he walked on through; his naturally distended stomach skimmed the surface of the forest floor, hobgoblinish, though it was actually a perfectly suitable arrangement, giving him a low and stable center of gravity. However, it was not a form that Earth folks could readily take to, these large webbed feet coming almost directly out of a low-hanging belly, and long hands trailing ape-fashion beside it. For this reason, he and his colleagues were million-years shy, and never had the inclination to make contact with anything other than the plant life of Earth. A failing, perhaps, but they'd monitored things long enough to know that to Earthmen their beautiful Ship was first of all a target and they themselves material for a taxidermist to display under glass.

So the extraterrestrial moved cautiously, quietly through the forest, eyes searching around—bulbous eyes, enormously convex, the kind you might find on a giant frog hopping along. He knew what chance such a frog would have for survival on a city street, and he rated his own about the same. As for giving instruction to humanity at some seat of international government—it was out of the question when your nose was like a bashed-in Brussels sprout and your overall appearance was like that of an overgrown prickly pear.

He waddled along, in perfect stealth, knuckles brushing the leaves. Let some other visitors from space, of more familiar form, be humanity's teachers. His only interest was a little redwood sapling he'd had his protruding eye on for some time, up ahead.

He stopped beside it, examined it carefully, then dug it out, murmuring to it in his gravelly space-tongue, words of weird, unearthly shape, but the redwood seemed to understand, and the shock to its root system was neutralized as it lay in his great creased palm.

He turned, and a faint light reached his eyes, light that attracted him, from the little suburb in the valley beyond the trees; he'd been curious about it for some time, and tonight would be the last night he could investigate, for tonight a phase of investigation ended. His Ship would leave Earth behind for an extended period, until the next great mutation in Earth vegetation, a period to be marked by centuries. Tonight would be the last chance he'd have to peek in the windows.

He crept out of the stand of redwoods and lowered himself to the edge of a fire road cut through the hillside. The sea of yellow house lights glowed tantalizingly. He crossed the fire road, stomach dragging through the low brush; on the long voyage back through space, he'd have something to offer his shipmates: the tale of this little adventure into the lights, a lone prickly pear on the human road. The ancient crinkle lines at his eyes smiled.

He tiptoed down the edge of the fire road, on great webbed feet with great long toes. Earth wasn't perfect for his form; he'd been wrought on a planet that made sense out of feet like this. Where he'd come from, things were more fluid, and you could sort of paddle along and only infrequently have to waddle on solid ground.

The houselights flickered below, and for a moment his own heart-light answered, glowing ruby red. He loved Earth, especially its plant life, but he liked humanity too, and as always when his heart-light glowed, he wanted to teach them, guide them, give to them the stored intelligence of millennia.

His shadow shuffled before him in the moonlight, head shaped like an eggplant on a long stalk of a neck. As for his ears, they were hidden in the folds of his head, like the first shy shoots of baby lima beans. No, Earth would have too good a laugh were he to walk up its aisle of world government. Not all the stored intelligence in the universe was enough when people were laughing at your pearish silhouette.

He kept it hidden in the moonlight, with faint mist attending it, and proceeded on down the road. Inside his head he received the warning signal from the Ship, but knew it was premature, knew it was to give the more clumsy-footed members of the crew time. But he—he swung one duck-webbed monster of a foot forward, and then the other. He was fast.

By any standard of speed on Earth, of course, he was impossibly slow, an Earth child could move three times as fast; one had almost run him down with a bicycle one terrible night. Close, very close.

But not tonight. Tonight he'd be careful.

He stopped, listened. The Ship's warning signal came on again, thumping in his heart-light—the code of alarm. The instrument fluttered lightly, calling for a roundup of all crew members, second preliminary message. But there was time enough for the swift; he waddled left, right, left, knuckles fairly swimming in the leaves, as he dragged along toward the edge of the town. He was old, but he moved well, faster than most ten-million-year botanists with feet like marsh ducks.

His great orbicular eyes rolled, scanning the town and the sky and the trees and the ground immediately ahead. No one was coming from any direction, only himself, coming in for one quick look at an Earthling, and then goodbye for several rounds in the beloved Ship, far from here.

His orbiting gaze jumped suddenly forward, down the fire road, where a shaft of moving light appeared, followed by another, twin lights racing toward him out of nowhere! Simultaneously, his heart-alarm went into the panic stage: all crew return, danger, danger, danger.

He stumbled backward, then sideways, disoriented by the advancing light, which was much faster than a bicycle, much louder, much more aggressive. The light was blinding now, harsh Earth light, cold and clear. He stumbled again and fell off the fire road into the brush, light streaking between him and his Ship, light cutting him off from the redwood forest and the clearing beyond it, where the Great Ornament hovered, waiting.

Danger, danger, danger...

His heart-light flashed wildly. He reached for the little redwood sapling that had fallen on the road, its roots crying out to him.

His long fingers advanced, and drew back in a blur as the blinding light struck, and then roaring engines. He rolled in the brush, frantically covering his heart-light with a loose branch. His great eyes snapped, taking in detail on all sides, but none more horrible than the sight of the little redwood sapling, crushed by the vehicles, young leaves mangled, its consciousness still crying out to him: danger, danger, danger.

Light and more light followed on the fire road, a road that had always been empty, but now echoed with the sound of vehicles, and human voices, shouting, raging, intent on capture.

He struggled through the brush, fluttering heart-light still hidden by his hand, while the cold light sought for him, sweeping the brush. All the star intelligence in seven galaxies could not help him move faster in the foreign element. His duckish toes, how absurdly useless they were; he felt the swiftness of human feet upon their own ground, advancing all around him, and knew what a fool he'd been to tempt them.

Their quick thumping sounded and cold streaks of light cut the brush, over and over. Their alien tongues bellowed, and one of their number, with much jingling at his waist, was on the scent. In the flashing light, the old botanist saw the man's belt, with something hanging from it like an assemblage of teeth, jagged-edged, trophies possibly, wrenched from the mouth of some other unfortunate space creature, and placed on a ring.

Time, time, time, called the Ship, rounding up its last straggling members.

He lunged under the surging lights, to the edge of the fire road.

The vehicles were scattered, as were the drivers. He turned on his protective mist and glided across the road in the moonlight, blending with the foul exhaust from their engines, the noxious cloud momentarily adding to his camouflage—and then he was across the road and sliding down a low ravine.

Just as quickly, their cold lights turned, as if sensing where he'd crossed. He huddled against the sand and rock, as the Earthmen leapt across the ravine. His orbiting eyes raced upward and he saw the horrible ring of jingling teeth, grinning hideously as its owner leapt over him.

He crouched deeper into the rock, mist around him, no different from other little patches of fog one sees in ravines, by night, where the moisture clings. Yes, I'm just a cloud, Earthlings, one of your own, insignificant, don't probe it with your lights, for there is a great long neck inside it, and two webbed feet with toes as long and spindly as the roots of a purplish toadshade plant. You wouldn't understand, I'm sure, that I'm on your planet to save your foliage before you completely annihilate it.

The others jumped over him, dark voices excited, enjoying the hunt and well armed.

He scampered up after the last one had passed and entered the forest behind them. His only advantage was his knowledge of this beloved terrain, from which he'd been gathering. His eyes revolved quickly, locating the trail, a faint indentation in the gathering of branches that netted the darkness, a path he and his crewmates had made while bearing the seedlings away.

The rough ungracious light stabbed the dark, shining at different angles. The Earthmen were confused now, and he was navigating directly along back to the Ship.

His heart-light grew brighter, the energy field of his group strengthening it as he neared them, all their hearts calling to him, as well as the hundred million years of plant life on board, calling *danger, danger, danger*.

He rushed between the sweeping lights, along the single clear path in the forest, his long toe-roots feeling each impression with exquisite sensitivity. Each tangle of leaves, each spiderweb was known to him. He felt their gentle messages, speeding him through the forest, saying *this way, this way...*

He followed, fingers trailing the soft floor, long roots dragging, wiggling, receiving signals from the forest—while his heart-light blazed, eager to merge with those hearts in the clearing where the great Ship waited.

He was ahead of the cold light now, its beams entangled in branches that had admitted him, but which denied his pursuers; branches sprang out, locked together, and blocked their passage; a low root lifted slightly, tripping the fellow with the ring of teeth, and another root trapped the foot of his subordinate, who fell face-flat on the ground, cursing in the tongue of the planet, while the plants cried run, run, run...

The extraterrestrial ran, through the forest to the clearing.

The Grand Ornament, Jewel of the Galaxy, waited for him. He waddled toward it, toward its serene and beautiful light, light of ten million lights. Its wondrous powers were all converging now, emitting supreme waves of radiance that reflected all around. He pushed along through the grass, trying to become visible to the Ship, to put his heart-light in touch, but his long, ridiculous toes were entangled in some weeds that wouldn't let go.

Stay, they said, stay with us.

He yanked loose and pushed forward, into the outermost aura of shiplight, just at the edge of the grass. The radiant ornament shone through the stalks all around him, casting its glorious rainbow. He spied the hatch, still open, and a crewmate standing in it, heart-light flashing, calling to him, desperately searching.

I'm coming, I'm coming...

He shuffled through the grass, but his hanging stomach, shaped by other degrees of gravity, slowed him, and a sudden group decision flooded him, a feeling that swept through his very bones.

The hatch closed, petals folding inward.

The Ship lifted off as he burst from the grass, waving his long-fingered hand. But the Ship couldn't see him now; its enormous power-thrust was being employed, blinding light obliterating all detail in the landscape. It hovered momentarily, then departed, spinning above the treetops, the lovely ornament returning to the outermost branches of the night.

The creature stood in the grass, his heart-light flashing with fear.

He was alone, three million light-years from home.

Mary sat in the bedroom, feet up, half reading a newspaper, half listening to the voices of her two sons and their friends, playing Dungeons & Dragons in the kitchen below.

"So you get to the edge of the forest, but you make a truly stupid mistake, so I'm calling in the Wandering Monsters."

Wandering Monsters, thought Mary, and turned her newspaper.

How about suffering mothers? Divorced, with low support payments. Living in a house with children who speak a foreign tongue.

"Can I get Wandering Monsters called out for just befriending a goblin?"

"The goblin was a mercenary for thieves, so be grateful you only have Wandering Monsters to deal with."

Mary sighed, folding her paper. Goblins, mercenaries, orks, you name it, she had it, down in her kitchen, night after night, as well as the rubble of a ruined city of Crush bottles, potato-chip bags, books, papers, calculators, and horrible oaths pinned to her memo board. If anyone knew in advance what it was to raise kids, they'd never do it.

Now the group broke into song:

> *"She was twelve when he yanked the plug.*
> *Fifteen reds and a jug of wine . . ."*

What a lovely song, thought Mary, her teeth gnashing at the thought of one of her own babies taking a handful of reds some night, or a handful of something else, LSD, DMT, XYZ, who knew what they'd come home with next? An ork, maybe?

"Steve's Dungeon Master. He's got Absolute Power."

Absolute power. Mary stretched out her aching feet and wiggled her toes. As head of the house, *she* should be the one with Absolute Power. But she couldn't even get them to dry a dish.

I feel like an ork.

She had only a vague notion of what the creature was like, but it seemed to approximate the way she felt. Orkish.

The subterranean voices continued with their deranged dream, directly under her bedroom.

"What are these Wandering Monsters?"

"Human," said the Dungeon Master.

"Hah. The *worst*. Listen to their qualities: Megalomania. Paranoia. Kleptomania. Shitzoid."

That's *schizoid,* said Mary toward the wallpaper.The way *I've* begun to feel. Have I raised my babies to be Dungeon Masters? For that, I work eight hours a day?

It wouldn't be so bad, maybe, if my own life were as—as spontaneous as theirs. With surprise calls from my admirers.

She went down the list of her admirers, but had to admit there was something orkish about them, too.

"Okay then, I run ahead of the humans and shoot just my little arrows at them to make them chase me. My lead arrows..."

My youngest son, thought Mary, listening to Elliott's thin, squeaky voice. My baby. Shooting lead arrows. She felt as if *she'd* been shot with one, right in the thyroid gland or whatever it was that ran her energy down into the pits where the orks lived. God, she needed a lift so badly...

"I run down the road. They're after me. Just when they're about to get me and they're really mad, I throw down my portable hole..."

Portable hole?

Mary leaned off the edge of the bed to hear some more about *that* one. It sounded faintly obscene.

"I climb in and pull the lid closed. Presto. Disappeared into thin air."

If only I had one, she thought. To climb into about four thirty every day.

"You can only stay in a portable hole for ten milli-rounds, Elliott."

All I need it for is about ten minutes at the office. And maybe a little later, in heavy traffic.

She swung her feet off the bed, in a firm resolution to face the evening squarely, without any anxiety symptoms.

But where was romance?

Where was the exciting male in her life?

He was waddling down the fire road. The road was silent now, his pursuers gone, but he could not last long in this atmosphere. Earth gravity would get to him, and the ground resistance twist his spine out of shape; his muscles would sag and he'd be found in a ditch somewhere with no more definition than a large bloated squash. What an end for an intergalactic botanist.

The fire road dipped and he followed it toward the lights of the suburb below. He swore at those lights, which had so fatally attracted him, and which attracted him now. Why was he descending toward them? Why did his toe-tips tingle and his heart-light flutter? What help could there be for him there, in alien circumstances?

The fire road ended in low shrubs and bushes. He crept through them stealthfully, keeping his head low, and holding one hand over his heart-light. It fluttered enthusiastically, and he cursed it too. "Light," he said to it in his own tongue, "you belong on the rear end of a bicycle."

The bizarre house-forms of Earth were directly ahead, held down by gravity, unlike the lovely floating terraces of—

It was bad to think of home. Such memories were torture.

The moth-light of the houses grew bigger, and still more compelling. He stumbled through the brush and down a sandy bluff, his long toes tracing outlandish tracks there, upon a winding path that led toward the houses.

Directly ahead of him was a fence he'd have to climb. Such long fingers and toes as he had were good for getting a grip...on...obstacles...

He climbed like a vine to the top of the fence, but toppled down the other side, stomach upward, feet flailing. He hit, limbs splaying in every direction, a whimper of pain on his lips, and rolled, pumpkinlike, across the lawn.

What am I doing here, I must be mad...

He braked himself and froze on the alien ground. The Earth house was awesomely near, its lights and shadows dancing before his terror-stricken eyes. Why had his heart-light led him here? Earth houses were grotesque, horrible.

But something in the yard was sending soft signals. He turned, and saw the vegetable garden.

Its leaves and stems moved in shy patterns of friendliness; sobbing, he crept toward them and embraced an artichoke.

Hiding in the vegetable bed, he took counsel with the plants. Their advice, to go look in the kitchen window, was not welcome.

I'm in all this trouble, he signaled the plant, because of wanting to peek in windows. I can't repeat such folly.

The artichoke insisted, grunting softly, and the extraterrestrial crept off obediently, eyes whizzing around in fearful circles.

The square of kitchen light radiated outward, ominous as any black hole in space. Vertigo filled his limbs as he dropped into this unspeakable vortex at the outermost edge of the universe. His eyes came up past a plastic weathervane with a mouse and a duck balanced on it. The duck was out, carrying an umbrella.

At a table in the middle of the room sat five Earthlings, engaged in ritual. The creatures were shouting, and moving tiny idols around on the table. Sheets of paper were waved, bearing dark secrets, for each Earthling kept hidden from the other what was printed there.

Then a powerful cube was rattled and tossed, and they all watched its six-sided form land, just so. Again they shouted, consulted their tablets, and moved their idols, as their alien tongues sounded in the night air.

"I hope you suffocate in your portable hole."

"Listen to this: Lunacy. Hallucinator insanity..."

"Yeah, read some more."

"This form of malady causes the afflicted to see, hear, and otherwise sense things which do not exist."

He sank down from the window into darkness again.

The planet was unspeakably strange.

Could he ever learn the ritual, throw the six-sided cube himself, and be accepted?

Vibrations of monstrous complexity floated out to him from within the house, intricate codes and signals given back and forth. He was ten million years old and had been a great many places, but he'd never encountered anything as complicated as this.

Overwhelmed, he crept away, needing to rest his brain in the vegetable patch. He'd peeked into Earth windows before, yes, but never from so close, never partaking so intimately of the bizarre thought patterns of the people.

But they are only children, said a nearby cucumber.

The ancient botanist let out a whimper. If what he'd just heard were the thought waves of children, what must those of the adults be like? What impenetrable intricacies awaited him there?

He slumped down next to a cabbage and lowered his head.

It was all over. Let them come in the morning, take him away, and stuff him.

Mary showered, attempting to revive herself. Then, wrapping her head in a towel, she stepped onto the bath mat, which Harvey the dog had chewed to pieces.

The ruined fringes played between her toes as she dried herself and slipped into her imitation-silk kimono. She turned to the mirror.

What new wrinkle, what tiny sag, what horrible erosion would she detect this evening, to complete her depression?

Damages seemed slight. But one never knew, one couldn't begin to anticipate the childhood atrocities that might overtake the house at any moment—fights, drugs, unbearably loud music—to hasten her physical and moral decay. She applied some outrageously expensive moisturizing cream and prayed for peace and quiet.

It was broken immediately by Harvey the dog barking his head off, from his exiled post on the back porch.

"Harvey!" She called out the bathroom window. "Shut up!"

The animal was ridiculously suspicious of things that passed in the dark; it made her feel the neighborhood was filled with sex fiends. If he'd bark *just* at sex fiends, he'd be useful.

But he barked at the Pizza Wagon, at airplanes, at faint satellites, and suffered, she feared, from Hallucinator Insanity.

Not to mention eating bath mats.

She yanked the window open again. "Harvey! For God's sake, pipe down!"

She slammed the window shut, and left the bathroom.

What lay ahead of her down the hall was not appealing, but she had to cope.

She opened the door to Elliott's room.

It was piled with objects of every sort of useless-ness, to the point of decay. A typical boy's room. She'd like to stuff it in a portable hole.

She began.

Organizing, discarding, filing: she hung his space-ships from the ceiling, rolled his basketball into the closet. She had no ideas for the stolen street sign. She hoped he wasn't anal or something. She suspected Elliott had much the matter with him, being fatherless, joyless, and having a penchant for hanging out with Wandering Monsters in his every free moment. Taken all around, he wasn't even nice.

But maybe it was just a *stage*.

"Elliott . . ." She called to her little ork.

Of course, there was no answer.

"Elliott!" She shrieked for him, thus raising her blood pressure and deepening the shriek-lines around her mouth.

Elliott's footsteps thundered on the stairs, then rumbled along the hall. He whipped around the door frame, all four feet of him, adorable in some respects, none of which were visible at the moment, as he looked suspiciously at what she'd done to his collec-tion of trash.

"Elliott, do you see what this room looks like right now?"

"Yeah, I won't be able to find anything."

"No dirty dishes, clothes put away. Bed made. Desk neat . . ."

"Okay, okay."

"This is what a mature person's room is supposed to look like all the time."

"Why?"

"So that we won't feel like we're living inside a litter basket. All right?"

"Yeah, all right."

"Is that a letter from your father?" Mary pointed to the desk, to the handwriting she knew so well, from all the Master Charge slips it'd appeared on. "What did he say?"

"Nothing."

"I see." She tried, casually, to change the subject. "You want to repaint in here? It's getting grungy."

"Sure."

"What color?"

"Black."

"Cute. A healthy sign."

"I like black. It's my favorite color."

"You're squinting again. Have you had your glasses off?"

"No."

"Mary!" The Dungeon Master called from below. *"Your song is on!"*

She leaned her head out the door. "Are you sure?"

"Your song, Mom," said Elliott. "Come on."

She heard, faintly, the sound of the Persuasions coming from the kitchen. She followed the beat, down the stairs, Elliott in front of her. "Did your father mention you guys coming for a visit?"

"Thanksgiving."

"Thanksgiving? He knows Thanksgiving is mine." But when had he ever been consistent? Except on the bottom line of charge slips, where he'd worn out numerous ballpoints. Buying parts for his motorcycle.

She thought of him, zooming somewhere, moonlight on his heavy-lidded eyes, and sighed. Oh, well . . .

She'd have Thanksgiving dinner at the Automat. Or the Chinese restaurant, the turkey stuffed with MSG.

Elliott ducked away from her, and Harvey started barking again, at an approaching car.

The extraterrestrial dove between rows of vegetables and flattened himself out there, arranging a few leaves over his protruding shape.

There's nothing to fear, said a tomato plant. It's only the Pizza Wagon.

Not knowing what a Pizza Wagon might be, the extraterrestrial remained in the leaves.

The Wagon stopped in front of the house. A door in the house opened and he saw an Earthling emerge.

That's Elliott, said the green beans. He lives here.

The extraterrestrial peeked over the leaves. The Earthling was only slightly taller than he was. But the Earthling's legs, of course, were grotesquely long and his stomach did not hang on the ground in the elegant manner of certain higher life forms—but he was not too terribly frightening to behold.

The boy went down the driveway and out of sight.

Go around the side, said the tomato. You'll get a good view of him returning.

But the dog—

The dog is tied, said the tomato. He ate Mary's overshoes.

The extraterrestrial scampered out of the vegetable patch and circled the house. But the lights of the Pizza Wagon suddenly swept the yard as it turned in the drive and he panicked; wrenching himself along, he leapt onto the fence and started to climb over. One of his long toes accidentally depressed the gate latch and he found himself swinging back into the yard.

The Earthling was near, was looking his way.

Quickly he covered his heart-light, dropped from the gate and dove into the toolshed, where he crouched, fearful mist surrounding him.

He'd trapped himself, but there were tools in the shed, a digging fork with which to defend himself. In many ways it resembled tools from his Ship, for gardening is gardening. He gripped its handle in his long fingers and prepared to meet his attacker. A cornered intergalactic botanist is not someone to trifle with.

Don't stab yourself in the foot, said a little potted ivy.

He braced. From the garden he felt the mental wave of a nearby orange tree, as one of its fruits was plucked by the Earth child.

A moment later the fruit hurtled into the toolshed, and struck him in the chest.

The little old being tumbled backward, sinking down on his large squashy bottom, the orange bouncing off him onto the toolshed floor.

How humiliating, a botanist of his stature, pelted with ripe fruit.

Angrily he grabbed the orange, wound up one of his long, powerful arms, and whipped it back into the night.

The Earthling cried out, and scampered away.

"Help! Mom! Help!"

Mary chilled all over. What acceleration of the aging process was she about to undergo?

"There's something out there!" shouted Elliott, bursting into the kitchen. He turned, slammed the door, and locked it.

Mary weakened deeply, looked at the Dungeons & Dragons display, and desperately wished for a portable hole large enough for all of them. What was she supposed to do now? It hadn't been mentioned in divorce court.

"In the toolshed," babbled Elliott. "It threw an orange at me."

"Oooooo," mocked Tyler the Dungeon Master, "sounds dangerous."

The boys got up from the game and headed for the door, but Mary got in front of them. "Stop. You all stay right here."

"Why?"

"Because I said so." She drew herself up, tossed her head bravely, and grabbed the flashlight. If it *was* a sex fiend, she'd go out and, like a mother partridge, offer herself as a decoy.

She just hoped he was a halfway charming fiend.

"You stay here, Mom," said Michael, her older boy. "We'll check it out."

"Don't get condescending with me, young man."

Alongside her, another of the Dungeon crowd, young Greg, had grabbed a butcher knife.

"Put that down," said Mary, and gave them her withering stare of Absolute Power. They pushed past her, opened the door, and rushed out into the yard.

She followed, hanging on to Elliott. "What exactly did you see?"

"In there." He pointed at the toolshed.

She shined her flashlight inside, onto pots, fertilizers, hoes, shovels. "There's nothing in there."

Michael's voice sounded across the lawn. "The gate's open!"

"Look at these tracks!" shouted the Dungeon Master, rushing toward the gate.

Their gross, tangled tongue meant nothing to him, but the ancient voyager could see their forms clearly now, from his hiding place on the sandy hillside. There were the five Earth children, and . . .

Who is that exotic creature with them?

His heart-light began to glow, and he quickly covered it over.

Deftly, he waddled closer, to see more of this tall, willowy being who accompanied the children.

She did not have a nose like a bashed-in Brussels sprout, nor the shape of a sack of potatoes, but . . .

He crept a little closer.

"Okay, party's over. Back in the house. Greg, give me that knife."

The clang-banging syllables of her language were meaningless to him, but he sensed that she was mother to this crew.

Where was the father, towering and strong?

She threw him out years ago, said the green beans.

"Here's the pizza," said Greg, picking it up. "Elliott stepped on it."

"Pizza? Who said you guys could order pizza?" Mary passed under the porch light, and the extraterrestrial gazed at her from his hiding place, thoughts of escape temporarily set aside.

Foolish heart-light, he said to that peculiar organ, which fluttered now. You belong on—on a Pizza Wagon.

Mary shooed them back into the house, satisfied that the worst had passed. Elliott had been fantasizing again, that was all, and had merely given his mother a few more frown lines. It did not justify grinding up small doses of Valium into his food each night. It was just a stage he was passing through.

"There was something out there, Mom, I swear."

Tyler mocked. "Douchebag, Elliott."

"Hey," said Mary, "no douchebag in my house." They knew too much; they were out past her at every turn. All she could hope for was some kind of stand-off, but she sensed it was impossible. "All right, everyone, time to go home."

"We didn't eat the pizza."

"It has footprints in it," said Mary, desperately

wishing to have quiet restored, but of course they ignored her, and began eating the stepped-on pizza. She dragged herself back toward the stairs, feeling quite stepped-on herself. She'd lie down, put some herbal pads on her eyes, and count iguanas.

She turned at the top of the stairs. "When that pizza's done, everyone out."

A rumbling grumble sounded from the Dungeon.

How nice it must have been when children went to work in coal mines at the age of nine. But those days, she felt, were gone forever.

She stumbled into her room, and collapsed on the bed.

Just another typical evening in the life of the gay divorcee.

Cold chills, shock, and Wandering Monsters.

She applied her eyepads and stared blindly toward the ceiling.

Something seemed to be staring back.

But that was just her overwrought imagination, she knew.

And if that damned dog doesn't stop barking, I'm going to leave him beside the highway with a note in his mouth.

She breathed deeply and began counting her lizards, each of them shuffling toward her in a friendly sort of way.

The Dungeons & Dragons game moved, stealthily, to the playroom, everyone playing but Elliott, who went to his own room, sulking. He fell asleep, with odd dreams disturbing him, of immense perspective patterns, lines angling in to form doorway after doorway, leading to...

...space. He ran through, but more doorways were always ahead.

He was not the only one in a strained mood: Harvey the dog chewed through his leash and snuck off his back-porch post. He tiptoed up to Elliott's room, slunk in, and pawed down; he contemplated Elliott's sleeping form, then contemplated Elliott's shoes, but eating them would only make waves. But he was nervous, ill at ease, needed distraction. He had not especially enjoyed his evening bark at the moon. Something weird had entered the yard and Harvey's fur had stood up straight, little whimpers escaping his snout until he'd pulled himself together and begun yapping in the expected fashion. What had been out there? He didn't know.

He began a halfhearted wash of tail-parts, soft tongue slurping, teeth rounding up a few fleas. Then suddenly, he heard the sound again.

Elliott heard it too, was sitting up in bed.

Harvey growled, fur standing stiffly, eyes darting fearfully about. He needed to bite someone, settled for skulking alongside Elliott, out the door of the bedroom, down the steps, and through the house to the backyard.

•   •   •

The elderly space-being had slept on the sandy hillside, but then had risen again and gone back toward the house.

The windows had all been dark. He'd found the gate latch, depressed it with his toe in the correct manner, and entered, much as an Earthling might. But his lumpish silhouette on the moonlit lawn told him he was far from being one of those creatures. For some odd reason, Earth stomachs had not evolved in the pleasantly round downward style his had, into a stomach of substance, a stomach in touch with the terrain. Earthlings were like luckless string beans, strung up on their latticework of bone and muscle to the very snapping point.

While he was a comfortable creature, low-slung and contemplative.

Musing in this manner, he waddled across the yard to have another strategy meeting with the vegetables. But his large foot depressed the hidden edge of a metal garden tool and its handle rose up toward him at a high rate of speed.

It struck him in the head and he fell backward with an intergalactic scream, then dashed into the little patch of corn nearby; moments later, the back door opened and an Earthling rushed out, with the cowering dog.

Elliott charged across the yard, flashlight on, and shone it into the toolshed.

The cold beam played over the tools again, and Harvey leapt into the fight, biting a hole in the peat bag, which made him feel much better, but left him with a mouthful of moss. He danced about, somewhat muffled, snapping at shadows.

In the corn patch, the extraterrestrial lay crouched, clutching a cucumber, ready to do battle. His teeth were grinding fearfully, and he trembled all over.

The cornstalks separated, the boy looked in, screamed, and dove to the earth.

The space creature backed off through the cornstalks and hurried for the gate, big feet flapping.

"Don't go!"

The boy's voice had the edge of gentleness in it, as young plants have—and the old botanist turned to look at him.

Their eyes met.

The dog of the house was racing in circles, barking, moss flying out of his mouth.

A peculiar diet, thought the elderly space-scientist, but did not linger to investigate further. Harvey's teeth flashed in the moonlight, but the boy collared the dog, crying again to the spaceman, "Don't go!"

But the ancient being was already going, out the gate and into the night.

Mary woke, beneath her eyepads, and felt the house was tilted somehow, on its side. She rose, put on a housecoat, and stepped into the shadows of the hall.

Voices came to her from the playroom. Often enough she wondered what they played at in there; posters of half-näked space princesses seemed essential to their pleasure.

My babies, she sighed to herself. Then, upon nearing the playroom, she heard Tyler's voice, and Steve's, and Greg's—The Dungeoners whom she'd specifically told to go home. Of course they'd ignored her command. Of course they were spending the night and would appear before their own mothers tomorrow, bleary-eyed, acting as if they'd slept in a brothel.

I can't take much more of this.

She tightened her housecoat and prepared to attack, but the door was half open and she saw flashing red light—their homemade laser show, in time to soft music.

The effect was soothing, she had to admit.

And wasn't it—creative?

"Look, it looks like a tit. There's the nipple."

She slumped against the wall. You couldn't win. If she went in there like a madwoman, if she imprinted them with the image of mature-woman-screaming-in-her-housecoat-somewhere-in-the-night, mightn't it inhibit their sexual development? And give them a complex?

Anyway, it'd certainly give her a headache.

Like a wounded camel, she slouched back into the shadows—just as Elliott bolted up the steps and rushed into the playroom.

"You guys?"

"Look at that—a *pair* of tits."

"There was a monster in the backyard!"

"A monster? Hey, I'm getting a real topless Martian together here."

"It was—a goblin! About three feet tall, with long arms. He was in the corn patch."

"Shut the door before you wake Mom."

The door closed. Mom walked slowly back toward her room. The house wasn't tilted on its side, Elliott was. Tilted all out of shape.

Either that, or a shy sex fiend had selected *her* vegetable garden in which to perform unnatural acts.

Why? she wondered.

Why me?

"It was here, right here..."

The extraterrestrial listened to the voices of the men, who still paced back and forth upon the landing site. Watching from the trees, he could infer the meaning of their speech: here a wondrous craft had been, and had escaped them. Here a Ship of Wonder, such as their planet could only gape at, had descended and taken off again.

"...and it slipped through my fingers."

The leader, bearing the jingling ring of teeth, turned, turned again. His subordinates nodded stupidly. Their leader entered his vehicle and departed, and they followed him. It was day and the landing site was empty.

The extraterrestrial stared mournfully at the traces the Ship had left.

It slipped through my fingers...

He raised a hand limply. Exhaustion had set in on him, and hunger. The powerful ration tablets he and his crewmates survived on—compressed little miracles of nutrition—were not of Earth. He had tried to chew a few bunch-berries, found them most unsatisfying, and spat out the hard little seeds. During ten million years of gathering wild plant life, he'd never found it necessary to learn which ones were nutritious, and it was late in the game to start now.

Oh, for one tiny ration tablet, loaded with energy.

He slouched back in the brush, weak, depressed, and itching all over from a species of trumpet-creeper he'd sampled. The end was near.

Elliott pedaled along the street toward the far hills. He did not know why. The headlight of his bike was like a magnet heading for iron, buried in the hills. Yes, the bike seemed to know where to go and he rode with it.

Elliott was what is generally called a twerp. He cheated at Parcheesi. He had a shrill, screeching voice that came and went like a genie in a bottle, but always said just the wrong thing, in class or at home during dinner.

Whatever he could avoid in life, he avoided, hoping Mary would take care of it for him, or Michael. There were other things, the list was long, including thick eyeglasses that made him feel like a frog in a bottle. All in all, a blossoming neurotic, a twerp. His path in life led nowhere, but if a place could be pointed to on a map of the soul, Elliott's destination was mediocrity, miserliness, and melancholy; the sort of person who falls under a train. Something of this sort awaited him a child psychologist would tell you, except that Elliott's path had veered today—into the hills.

He followed the bike's urgings, up to the fire road. He climbed off and walked it over the cut foliage. His bike was dented and rusty from his having tossed it aside so often, abandoning it to rain, but today it seemed light as a feather. Today it seemed to shine like new, right through the rust.

It led him through the forest, along a winding path. Elliott came to the clearing, and knew something incredible had been there. Everything seemed to bear the memory of the Great Ship. Squinting through his glasses at the imprinted grass, he could almost discern the shape the Ship had been.

Elliott's heart was beating loudly, and were there a light in it, it would have been on. His forehead seemed to be on fire, caught in the afterglow of an immense power that still lingered in the clearing.

The old space being in the nearby bushes did not reveal his presence, for the boy's unpleasant dog might be sniffing about too, with hopes of biting a distinguished scientist on the ankle.

But no—the youth seemed to be alone. Still, it was best to remain unnoticed. An extraterrestrial was about to expire in the underbrush and there was no point in involving strangers.

The boy, however, proceeded with a peculiar series of acts. He brought a bag from his pocket, from which he took a tiny object. He placed the object on the ground, walked a few paces, placed another, and another, and another, until he was out of sight, far along a hidden path.

The ancient traveler crawled feebly from the bushes. Curiosity was his worst character trait, but he was too old to change now. On hands and knees, he entered the clearing to see what the youth had deposited there.

It was a small round pill, bearing a remarkable resemblance to a space-nutrition tablet. He turned it over in his palm. Upon it was printed an indecipherable code:

M & M

He put it in his mouth and let it dissolve.
Delicious.
In fact, exquisite. Indeed, he'd never tasted anything like it anywhere in the galaxy.

He hurried along the trail, eating one pill after another, strength returning, hope surging in his heart. The trail led him to the boy's house once more.

Mary served dinner. It was one of her better meals: raw wheat germ sprinkled on canned macaroni and cheese, with a handful of cashews tossed in to give a last touch of class. "Eat your supper, Elliott."

He was hunched as always over the main course, as if preparing to snorkel his way into it.

I have raised a depressed child.

Mary's mind flashed to previous dinners, those of another period, when Elliott was younger and she and her husband had thrown butter knives at each other. An entire chicken had bounced off the wall, and mashed potatoes had hung from the ceiling like stalactites, dripping gravy onto Elliott's tender young head. It could not have been good for him. She tried to brighten this present meal with chatter.

"Well, how is everyone going to dress up for Halloween?" The dread evening was approaching fast; her house would be visited by several hundred children singing off key, and then staring at her.

"Elliott's going as a goblin," said Michael.

"Up yours," snarled Elliott.

"Young man—" Mary rapped her fork on Elliott's glass "—eat your macaroni."

"Nobody believes me," said Elliott, and gazed still more glumly into their gay repast. Mary stroked his hand.

"It's not that we don't believe you, honey..."

"It was real, I swear." Elliott looked at her from behind his thick lenses, over-large eyes filled with pleading.

Mary turned to Gertie, the last child in the family, five years old and already asking for her own apartment. "Gertie, honey, what are you going as on Halloween?"

"Bo Derek."

The image of her infant daughter parading naked and wet down the block flooded Mary's taxed mind. She fumbled with her macaroni and tried to think of another subject, but Michael was circling back in on Elliott.

"Maybe," said Michael, in his superior-brother way, "it was an iguana."

"I've got the iguanas," said Mary softly, into a cashew.

"It was no iguana," said Elliott.

"Well," said Michael, "you know how there are supposed to be alligators in the sewers?"

Alligators, thought Mary. I could start counting alligators. As a change.

She closed her eyes and a great big one appeared, teeth sparkling.

She turned back to Elliott. "Elliott, all your brother is saying is that you probably just imagined it. This happens. We all imagine lots of things, all the time..."

I imagine myself entering the sale rack and finding a displaced Dior, for two dollars. I make a stunning entrance, into McDonald's.

"I couldn't have imagined it," said Elliott.

"Maybe," said Michael, "it was a pervert."

"Please, Michael," said Mary, "don't imprint Gertie with that sort of talk."

"What's a pervert, Mommy?"

"He's just a man in a raincoat, honey."

"Or," continued Michael, "a deformed child."

"Michael..." She gave him her *silencio* look. Why

were children's minds so enamored of freakish explanations? Why was every dinner conversation like this? Where was the elegant banter of refinement, as the second course, frozen fish sticks, was served?

"Well," persisted Michael, ignoring her order for silence as he ignored all her other orders, "maybe it was an elf, or a leprechaun."

Elliott threw down his fork. "It was nothing like that, penis-breath!"

Penis-breath? Mary sat back, eyes wide.

How had *that* expression come into her little family circle?

All the elements of the expression came to her slowly, then, and she had to admit it was an organic possibility, one that could even produce a certain wistfulness in a lonely divorcee's mind, but—

"Elliott, you are never to use that expression at the dinner table again. Or anywhere else in this house."

Elliott slouched back into the tablecloth. "Dad would have believed me."

"Why don't you call him and tèll him?" If his phone is still connected, which I doubt.

"I can't," said Elliott. "He's in Mexico, with Sally."

Mary maintained her poise, sagging only a little way into the fish sticks as the name of her former friend, now hated enemy, was invoked. Children can be so cruel, she reflected. Especially Elliott.

"If you see it again, whatever it was, don't go near it. Call me and we'll have someone take it away."

"Like the dogcatcher?" asked Gertie.

"Exactly."

Harvey growled softly on the back porch, where he was chewing the welcome mat.

"But," said Elliott, "they'll give it a lobotomy or do experiments or something."

"Well," said Mary, "it should learn to stay out of other people's cucumbers."

However, it was crawling from the trees, as the town slept. It had never heard of lobotomy, but it had reason to fear being stuffed.

The aged creature's toes carried him along quietly, toward the boy's house. Down the hillside he went, leaving the mark of a large melon being dragged by a pair of duckbilled platypuses. The boy's house was dark, only one tiny window glowing.

He peered over the fence, great eyes rolling up, down, around. The dog was nowhere in sight.

Let me just get my toe up on the latch, in the accepted fashion . . .

. . . and then, swing in on it.

The great M&Ms have given me my vitality back. A miraculous food. The Ship would return in a thousand years; if the M&Ms held out, perhaps he'd make it.

Stop dreaming, you old fool.

You'll never get back—there.

He looked at the sky, but not for long, for the sadness written in it was too great. No amount of M&Ms would keep him going if the love of his shipmates was gone from his sight.

Why had they deserted him?

Couldn't they have held on a moment longer?

He closed the gate behind him with his foot, as he'd seen the boy do. He must learn these ways of Earth if he was to succeed.

He tiptoed across the backyard. To his surprise, he found the boy asleep in a sack beside the vegetables.

The child was breathing lightly. A faint mist escaped his lips, for the night was cold.

The extraterrestrial shivered himself, and his own mist poured out of his toes, mists of worry, fear, confusion.

Suddenly the boy's eyes opened.

Elliott looked up into enormous eyes, eyes like moon jellyfish with faint tentacles of power within them, eyes charged with ancient and terrible knowledge, eyes that seemed to scan every atom of his body.

The extraterrestrial stared down, horrified by the boy's protruding nose and large, exposed ears, and worst of all, by his tiny little eyes, dark and beady as those of a coconut.

But the tiny sunken eyes of the child blinked, and the terror in them touched the old scientist's heart. He extended a long finger.

Elliott shrieked and scrambled backward, clutching his sleeping bag around him; the extraterrestrial jumped in the other direction, stumbling over himself and emitting an ultrasonic squeak, which brought a bat sweeping down out of the darkness, but only momentarily, for one pass at the space monster sent the aerial rodent fluttering back into the night, teeth chattering.

Elliott's own teeth were clicking like a bagful of marbles, while his knees clacked back and forth and the hair stood up on his neck.

Where was Harvey the Protector, dog of the hearth?

On the back porch, teeth clicking, knees clacking, fur standing up. The terrified beast crouched, sprang at the door, bounced back and chased his tail; the scent he had in his nose was like nothing he'd ever sniffed before, with aromas of far-flung spaces no sane dog would ever want to investigate. He crouched back down, only the tip of his snout sticking out through a crack in the door; more of the scent floated toward him and he cringed, and began chewing the end of a broom.

The creature from space was taking another tentative step toward Elliott. Elliott's eyes widened in terror and he stepped backward. He had zero courage, had errands to run, homework to do, chores to perform, a thousand things, anything but this—

Monstrous eyes scanned his nature; he could feel the probes far down in himself, shooting energy through him, questioning, calculating, analyzing. The hideous creature's lips were shaped in a frightening grimace, sharp little teeth grinding together. What did it want? Elliott felt it trying to communicate.

The ancient wanderer held out his hand and opened

it. Within the huge scaly palm was his last M&M, melting.

Elliott looked down at the little candy, then looked up at the monster. The monster pointed a long finger into his palm, then pointed to his mouth.

"Okay," said Elliott, softly. He opened his jacket, took out his bag of M&Ms, and backed slowly away, continuing to lay a trail across the yard. His knees were still knocking and his teeth still clicking violently, upsetting some expensive orthodontic work.

The elderly space traveler followed, picking up each M&M and swallowing it down hungrily. This was the food of the gods, of kings, of conquerors. Were he to survive his ordeal on Earth, he would bring a sample of this miraculous food to his Captain, for with it vast universes could be crossed, in supreme flight.

Chocolate dribbled from the corners of the spaceman's mouth; his fingers were coated with it too. He licked it off deliriously, his strength returning; he could feel the miraculous substance coursing through his veins, bearing its secret chemistry to his brain, where blips of joy and light were going off. Now he understood the meaning of Earth life: ten billion years of evolution to produce—the M&M.

What more could one ask of a planet?

Grabbing at the little pills, he tracked his way quickly across the lawn, and before he knew it, he had followed the trail into the Earthling's house.

His eyes revolved in terror. The alien world surrounded him on all sides now—each corner, each object, every shadow was a devastating shock to his system. But he had to endure it, in order to acquire the miraculous M&M.

He followed the trail up a flight of stairs and down a hallway to the boy's room.

There the child rewarded him with a handful of M&Ms. He devoured them in one gulp. It seemed a rash act, but who knew what tomorrow would bring?

The boy's voicebox sounded.

"I'm Elliott."

The words were a jumble, incomprehensible. But anyone who would share their M&Ms could be trusted. The extraterrestrial sank down on the floor, exhausted. A blanket came around him and he slept.

Elliott lay awake for a long while, not daring to sleep. The monstrosity was on the floor beside his bed, grotesque shape outlined beneath the blanket. Where had it come from? He only knew that it wasn't from this earth.

He fought to understand, but it was like trying to take a handful of fog. Waves of power filled the room, visible the way heat in the desert is visible—in a shimmering dance that rises upward. Within that shimmer, Elliott felt a brilliant awareness moving; even while the creature slept, a sentry seemed to watch in its shimmer, and to study the room, and the windows, and the night.

A low whine from the hallway told Elliott that

Harvey had slipped off the back porch again, and that the dog was crouched outside his door. He heard a gnawing sound of teeth on the door frame, and the thump-thump of the dog's tail.

What's in there? the perplexed canine was asking himself as he nervously chewed wood. The shimmer that Elliott saw was touching him too, probing his muddled dog-thoughts. The cur whimpered and pawed the door, then sank back down, not really wanting to be let in, not wanting to get any closer to the shimmering wave that pulsed like an old bone—a choice bone, an ancient bone, but one of the frightening sort, with thunder in the marrow.

Elliott turned on his side, and put one arm under his pillow. Sleep was after him, though he wanted to watch, to stand guard. But his eyelids were heavy and he was sliding into home plate, sliding, sliding, down, down, down.

He landed on a Parcheesi board, the one he cheated on, and his feet seemed mired in it. But then he saw a trail of little candies, each one glowing like gold, the trail of M&Ms he'd laid for his monstrous friend, and the trail became a beautiful road through the world, and he took it.

The extraterrestrial woke next morning, not knowing what planet he was on.

"Come on, you have to hide."

The space creature was pushed across the room into a closet and shut in behind its louvered door.

In a few more minutes the rest of the house woke. The creature heard the voice of an older boy, and then that of the mother.

He huddled in the closet as the mother entered and spoke.

"Time for school, Elliott."

"I'm sick, Mom..."

The extraterrestrial peeked through the louvers of the closet door. The boy had returned to bed, and seemed to plead with the tall, willowy creature. She placed a tube in the boy's mouth and left the room. The boy quickly held it up to the light above his bed, heated the fluid within it, and placed it back in his mouth as the mother returned.

The old scientist nodded. A trick known around the galaxy.

"You have a temperature."

"I guess I do."

"You waited outside last night for that thing to come back, didn't you?"

The boy nodded.

The woman turned toward the closet. The extra-terrestrial shrank back into the corner, but only her hand entered, going to a quilt that lay above him on a shelf. She placed it upon the boy. "Think you'll live if I go to work?"

She thought he was probably conning her again, but he had been having some rough nights lately; she hoped it wasn't weird drugs that were making him crazy. His eyes looked a little strange, but his father's eyes had been frequently dilated, with delusions of one thing and another. Maybe it was hereditary. "Okay," she said, "you can stay home. But no TV, understand? You are not to disintegrate in front of the box."

She turned and went through the doorway, then paused, looking down at the door frame. "Has that damn dog been chewing up here again? I'm going to have his teeth capped with rubber."

She marched off down the hall, but after a few

steps she tilted, as if a wave had washed over her; she steadied herself and felt her forehead. A faint ripple ran across it, like fairy fingertips touching her. But a moment later it was gone.

She opened Gertie's door. "Rise and shine..."

The child sat up, blinking, then cheerfully put her legs over the side of the bed. "I was dreaming about the pervert, Mommy."

"Oh, really?"

"He had a long, funny neck and big, bulging eyes..."

"Was he wearing a raincoat?"

"He wasn't wearing anything."

It certainly sounds like a pervert, thought Mary, but she couldn't slow down for further speculation. "Time for breakfast. You go and help Michael."

She continued onward into the bathroom, for a brief morning wash with some ridiculously expensive soap that melted faster than ice; the bar, full-sized two days ago, was now a teensy-weensy, transparent sliver. But a friend had told her it prevented wrinkles, blemishes, pimples, and warts.

She lathered up, the soap vanished completely, and that was that, another six-dollar bar of nothingness down the drain.

She dried off—and a dream of the recent night rose out of her morning fog: a dream about a man, but a very *short* man, with an enormous potbelly and a funny, waddling walk.

Must be the pervert.

She continued on toward breakfast, which was the

usual blur, and then out of the house to the driveway, where Michael was practicing his driving, backing the car toward the street.

"Here you go, Mom," he said, stepping out.

"Thank you, dear," she said, getting behind the wheel and gripping it with her regular grim determination; she popped the clutch, gave it too much gas, and squealed away from the house, Michael cheering her.

Elliott, hearing the departure, got out of bed and opened the closet door. The extraterrestrial shrank back.

"Hey, come on outa there," said Elliott, extending his hand.

Reluctantly, the old monstrosity waddled forward, out of the closet, and looked around. A wide variety of objects met his gaze, all of them queer-shaped, most of them plastic. The only familiar item was a desk, but too high for one with such short legs as his own. And did he think he might write a letter and mail it to the moon?

"What am I gonna call you?" Elliott looked into the great flashing eyes of the monster, where tiny blossoms of energy kept blooming and fading, to be replaced by others. The creature was sensing his way around, and Elliott stood back to give him room. "You're an extraterrestrial, right?"

The extraterrestrial blinked, and Elliott felt the

great orbs answering him somehow, but the message was just a buzzing in his brain, as if a fly were inside his head.

Elliott opened the bedroom door. The monster jumped back, for the nasty little beast of an Earth-dog slavered on the other side, stupid curiosity in his eyes, unfriendliness on his tongue.

"Harvey! Be good! Don't bite or anything. Nice dog. Nice Harvey..."

"...errrrrggggggggg...errrrrrrrggggggggggg..."

The dog's speech was lower down the communication chain than the boy's, sounding like a space cruiser stuck in reverse.

"See, Harvey? He's okay. He won't hurt you. See?"

A faint wisp of mist came from the monster's toe. Harvey put his nose into the mist and saw dog-dimensions he wasn't prepared for: a great soup bone of light, hurtling through the night, flashing, flashing, with a howling sound descending into ancient echo chambers of space.

The dog cringed, his mind reeling. A fearful moan came from his lips. He backed off, nose down.

The monster came forward.

"Do you talk?" Elliott snapped his fingertips up and down like a yakking mouth.

The elderly scientist blinked again, then moved his own fingertips, making galactic-intelligence patterns, the cosmic super-codes of survival, ten million years' worth.

Elliott blinked stupidly, as the whizzing fingertips described delicate orbits, spirals, angles of physical law.

The old creature dropped his hands in frustration, seeing that nothing was grasped, and recollecting again that this was just a ten-year-old child.

Well, what am I supposed to do? The aged monster studied the situation. His brain was evolved so far past the boy's powers of comprehension, he could barely think where to begin.

I'm too specialized, thought the monster. Let me see, let me see . . .

He tried to scale himself down to the crude bumblings of Earth mentation, but wound up merely twiddling his digits. How could he hope to sign the great equations, those supreme insights born of wandering super-segments of time? He could barely ask for an M&M.

Elliott walked over to the radio, turned it on.

"You like this tune? You like rock 'n' roll?"

A sound such as the space-wanderer had never heard before was pouring out of the radio; telepathically, he received the image of rocks rolling down a hillside. He covered his sensitive ear-flaps with both hands and crouched low.

Elliott looked around, trying to think of other important things a creature from space should know about. He fished a quarter out of his bank. "Here's some of our money."

The ancient traveler stared at the boy and tried to

comprehend his speech, but the tongue of Earth was a blur of dull articulation.

"Here, see—it's a quarter."

The object offered was small, flat, round, with a shiny coating, different-hued from the M&M, but possibly this was even stronger survival food.

He bit down.

A piece of junk.

"Yeah, right," said Elliott, "you can't eat that. Hey, are you hungry again? I'm hungry, let's go have something to eat. Harvey..." Elliott admonished the dog. "...out of the way."

Harvey whined and tiptoed aside, then followed Elliott and the monster downstairs to the kitchen. He crouched by his dog-bowl and signaled Elliott that he wanted some Alpo to settle his nerves, a whole canful, which he'd gobble down in one bite. But Elliott ignored the request and Harvey had to settle for toothing the edge of his dish.

Elliott was opening drawers, taking out the ingredients of his favorite breakfast. "Waffles," he said, and started stirring up some batter. "They're my specialty. You ever have them?"

The elderly botanist watched as peculiar items appeared, none related to space travel. He watched, great eyes revolving, taking in increments of incomprehensible action, except that a long tentacle of goo was flowing off the cupboard onto the floor.

Harvey, in the manner of a wet mop, quickly tongued up the spilled batter, while Elliott managed to get the rest of it into the waffle iron. "There, see? It's cooking."

The old monster's nose twitched and he waddled over to the waffle iron. It smelled delicious, like a large M&M.

Elliott removed the finished waffle and opened other cupboards and drawers. "...syrup, butter, canned fruit, and how about a little whipped cream to top it off?"

The monster jumped as the ozone moved and the boy's hand erupted in a white stream.

"Don't be afraid, this is a good dish." Elliott put an M&M atop the whipped cream and handed the waffle to the hoary old time traveler. "And here's a fork. You know how to use one of these?"

The aged scientist looked at its sparkling tines. It was the best piece of machinery he'd seen so far in the house. Soft lights came to his mind. Yes, an object with four prongs...attached...to what? For an instant he felt his escape mechanism flash, deep in his mind, where its image was slowly forming.

"Hey, you eat with it. See? Like this, like I'm doing..."

The scientist fumbled, but managed to scoop up the M&M. He ate it and proceeded to the white cream below, tasting astounding chemical arrangements, crossed and crisscrossed, their formulas signaling him as he forked on, like eating one's way through a cloud. Excellent, excellent stuff...

"How about some milk? Here, have a glass."

The fluid danced about, jumping out on his fingers,

and his lip arrangement did not easily admit the shape of the glass, so he poured most of it on his chest, in a stream that ran over his heart-light area.

"Boy, you don't know anything, do you?"

The old voyager stared at the fork again, while spearing pieces of the crusty food. Four tines, sounding, click, click, click...

"What's the matter? You make me feel so sad all of a sudden."

Elliott's whole body swayed, caught in the high, powerful wave that had spilled over him; emotions he couldn't comprehend filled him up to the brim, as if he'd lost something incredibly wonderful that should have been his, always.

Click, click, click...

The aged creature had his own eyes closed in contemplation of the heights. Might there be an ear, immense distances away, listening to the song of four tines? But how? How could the universe be crossed by this small instrument? The elderly botanist wished he'd paid more attention to the talk of the navigators and communication crew, for they knew more of these subjects than he.

"We're going to have fun," said Elliott, shaking off the sadness and taking hold of the old monster's hand. "Come on..."

The long, rootlike fingers entwined with his, and Elliott felt he was leading a child younger than himself, but then the rippling wave washed over him again, bearing star-secrets and cosmic law, and he knew the creature was older than he was, by a great deal. Something altered inside Elliott, turning just slightly, like a gyroscope that mysteriously rights itself; he blinked, amazed at the feeling, the feeling that he was a child of the stars too,·and had never done anything to hurt anybody, ever.

He led the waddling monster back to the staircase. Harvey followed, dog-dish in his teeth, in case any loose kibble might be discovered along the way.

Elliott led the parade into the bathroom and over to the mirror, for he wondered if the creature had ever seen himself that way, in a looking glass. "See? That's you."

The venerable star-rover looked at his image in the crude reflective glass of Earth. His higher communication patterns were not visible, could not be seen rainbowing above his head in brilliant, subtle waves. The handsomest part of his visage was gone.

"Okay, this is a hand..." Elliott held up the appendage. The space fossil followed suit, lifting his own in an elementary movement of the higher category, his fingers twinkling formulas of high-speed rocketry, interstellar shortcuts, and cosmic prophecy.

"Boy, have you got weird fingers..." The child blinked, in slow Earth fashion, studying the digits themselves instead of their subtle signaling. Ah, me, sighed the star-wizard, he is dumber than a cucumber.

"This is where our water comes from," said Elliott, turning the faucets. "See, hot. Cold. How about that. Do you have running water where you come from?"

The old being took a handful of water and raised it to his face. His eyes shifted into microfocus and he tracked for a moment out of habit, into the world of tiny aquatic forms.

"You like water, huh? Look at this, this is great."

Elliott turned on the faucets in the bathtub and motioned the extraterrestrial to get in. "Go on, it won't kill you."

The archaic wanderer leaned over the tub, which was much like the study-tanks on the Great Ship, where a scientist might recline and explore the inner aquatic universe. In a fit of melancholy, he entered the tub.

A bell sounded. The scientist jumped in his bath, great feet splashing. Was he being secretly monitored by the water? Was this the laboratory, then, in which his own waves were to be measured?

"Relax, it's just the telephone..."

Elliott left the room and the creature submerged himself in the tub of water, calmed by its flow, comforted by the dance of its microorganisms. He closed down his breathing apparatus to the standby system and stretched out, completely underwater. He entered atomic focus and began reviewing the water molecule, watching its latent heat force. Could he use it somehow to aid himself?

Harvey the dog edged cautiously toward the tub. Some of his worst moments had been in there, during the annual flea-bath; he peered over the edge at the present occupant of the tub, who seemed to have more liking for it. Harvey was reminded of a large old snapping turtle he'd once attempted to mug; that meeting had turned out badly, a terrible bite on the nose being the final outcome. Thus the dog's reluctance to do more than just gaze at the submerged guest. Was Elliott going to shampoo him?

Elliott returned, looked down, and yanked the creature up. "Hey, you can drown doing that sort of thing!"

Harvey saw there'd be no shampooing. The guest apparently had no fleas.

"Are you part aquatic elf?" asked Elliott.

As long as he's not part snapping turtle, thought Harvey, and placed a paw gingerly over his own nose, just in case.

"Here's a towel, you know how to use one? Towel?"

The veteran of the supernova stared stupidly at the item, his own skin having a water-repellent sheath. He took the towel, looked at it, looked at the boy.

"Here, dry yourself off, dumbbell . . ."

The boy's hands touched him. Earthly fingers tinged with healing components entered his aching back. Thank you, young man, that is very kind of you.

"See, we each have our own towel. That's mine—" Elliott pointed "—that's Michael's, that's Gertie's, that's Mom's. That one used to be Dad's. He's down in Mexico. You ever fly there?"

The monster blinked, receiving a sad wave of feeling from the boy's communication band. The boy stepped closer, and spread his arms like wings. "You fly all kinds of places in your ship, right? You have a ship?"

The Ship, shining softly, appeared in the space

being's mind, lavender light beaming around its hull where the ancient inscriptions were carved. His own light, of the heart, gave a tiny glow in response, and now the boy's sadness was his own.

"You keep that towel," said Elliott. "That's yours. We'll mark it E.T., for extraterrestrial." He touched the monster again, amazed by the texture of the skin. Another wave went through Elliott and he knew that the creature was older than Methuselah, older than old. "You're something like a snake too, aren't you. Boy, you are really weird."

The scientist felt the boy's energy going *doop-doop-doop* down his inner channels; most interesting, these Earth forces, crude but kindly, if you gave them half a chance.

The monster signaled back with his own fingers, explaining the structure of the atom, the love of the stars, and the origin of the universe.

"You hungry again? How about some Oreo cookies?"

Harvey nodded and wagged his tail. Oreos were fine by him—not his favorite food, but a dog who eats the ends off brooms is not fussy. He toothed his dish and held it out to Elliott, who walked on by, leading the monster.

All right, thought Harvey, I'll just tag along.

He followed them down the hall to Elliott's room, where cookies were dispensed to the goblin. Harvey growled and thumped his dish.

"You're too fat, Harvey."

Fat? The dog turned in profile, to show his ribs.

But his ability to con Elliott was slipping; the monster was Elliott's pet now. Harvey sought what nutrition remained in one of Elliott's hiking boots.

Across the room, Elliott was opening the closet door and addressing the monster. "We've got to fix you a place in the closet. Make it like the space shuttle, okay? With everything you need."

But the elderly interstellular was staring up at the skylight of the room. Stretched across it was a painted dragon, wings spread outward and soft shafts of sunlight shining through it.

"You like that? Here, here are some more."

Elliott opened a book on the floor, and he and the monster looked at it.

"These are goblins... these are gnomes..."

The monster's eyes went through a series of focusing arrangements, including one that revealed the origin of the fibers composing the paper and back out again, to the painted, potbellied little creature, not altogether unlike himself, staring up from the page.

Had other travelers been stranded here, long ago?

Elliott left the creature to look at pictures, and began arranging the closet with pillows and blankets. He had not stopped to ask himself why he was harboring the monster, or what it meant; he'd been flying on automatic pilot, without questions, without doubling back on himself, without trying to duck out. He knew this thing had been handed to him from the stars, and he had to follow or—die.

"You'll like it in here," he called through the door. His mind and body moved almost without effort, signals pulsing inside him. He couldn't know that a cosmic law had touched him, gyrating him in a new direction; he only knew he felt better than he'd ever felt before.

Harvey the dog did not feel the same metamorphosis of being; gnawing on boot heels did little for his soul, still less for his stomach. He contented himself with the thought of biting the mailman on the ankle, an event scheduled for midmorning.

Elliott went down the hall and came back with a bowl of water, which gave Harvey momentary hope, but the bowl was placed in the closet, with instructions to the goblin. "That's for you, and the whole thing is your command module."

Elliott lined up a number of stuffed animals at the mouth of the door. "That's protective camouflage. You stay in line with them, nobody'll know the difference."

The bewildered old super-being stared dumbly at the arrangements.

Harvey stared too, a faint desire moving in him, to gnaw the head off a teddy bear.

Elliott stepped forward with a desk lamp. "Light. See?"

He switched it on, and the harsh glare of its crude interior assaulted the voyager's supersensitive eyes. He backed up, into a record player, his arm scraping the needle across the record. In spite of the unpleasant scratching sound, soft lights went off inside him, and again he was filled with developing blueprints for escape—using a fork, and—and something that turns, like this thing I've just bumped into. It will turn, and it will scratch . . . a message . . .

He gazed at the record player, seeking his solution there, as his own inner wheels turned, bearing all that he knew of communication devices.

He stumbled around, looking for other bits of hardware. He opened the desk drawer, tumbled its contents on his feet.

"Hey," said Elliott, "take it easy. I'm supposed to keep this place neat."

The wanderer explored other parts of the room, dumping, tossing, seeking. He must examine it all, and it was all so strange, from this primitive planet's groping creativity. Where was he to find his inspiration?

He stared up at a poster tacked to the wall, of a half-naked Martian space-princess, clad in loose bits of shining metal.

Hmmmmmmm . . .

He contemplated her for some moments, her ray-gun, her helmet, her electric boots.

"You like her?" asked Elliott.

The old voyager slowly lowered his hands, in, then out again, describing the more classic form of beauty, the downward-sloping pear-shape.

"We don't have too many like that around here," said Elliott. Then he put his hand to the old monster's elbow and led him gently toward the closet. "You stay in there, okay? Stay . . ."

The time-worn traveler shuffled into the little enclosure. He who had once supervised the plant life in the grandest mansions of space was being closeted with a skateboard.

He slumped down. Where was his Ship, the Wonder of the Universe, now that he needed her?

He received the sudden light of a beacon, deep in space, sweeping toward him, searching Earth from incalculable ranges.

"See," said Elliott, "there's even a little window in here."

He pointed to the small square of glass above the monster's head. "And here's your reading lamp." He switched it on. "Okay, I'll see you later. I'm gonna buy some more cookies and things."

The closet door shut. The voyager squinted at the harsh light from the lamp, then took a red handkerchief from the closet shelf and placed it over the lampshade. The light softened to a pastel pink, a glow like that of the Mother Ship.

He must signal it, must let his crewmates know that he lived.

The image of the fork came into his brain again, four tines trailing in a circle, click, click, click.

Mary pulled the car into the drive, fender lightly brushing the ashcans and sending them into an overturned pile. What did it matter, she was home. She turned off the ignition and just sat for a moment behind the wheel, mind and body exhausted. Maybe she needed ginseng. Or maybe just gin.

She opened the door and crawled out. Her gaze traveled up to Elliott's closet window, where he'd placed one of his stuffed goblins.

The things they make for children these days are enough to *cause* hallucinations.

She continued up the walk and onto the porch. Harvey met her at the door, bowl in his mouth.

"Don't give me that look, Harvey, I have enough guilt."

She pushed on past the pleading beast, to the mail table.

Any letters from secret admirers? Wandering Monsters?

Nothing, just junk, bills, overdue bills, long-overdue bills, and a letter from a collection agency. Let them break her kneecaps.

She tossed the mail in the conveniently situated wastepaper basket, and removed her shoes.

She called to her tribe. "Anybody home?" She received no answer, except from Harvey. "Take that bowl out of your mouth."

She remained in the hall chair, too tired to proceed further. A fly buzzed around her forehead and she brushed it away, then brushed it away again, then saw there wasn't any fly, and the buzzing was—in her head.

Next it'd be bells, and then—voices.

"Well, no time for a nervous breakdown today." She got up and proceeded to the kitchen, where she saw that Elliott had cooked a healthy breakfast for himself, on the floor. She cleaned off the cupboards, the doors, and then made herself a cup of strong coffee.

She sat with it for a long time, contemplating her feet. Tired feet. Feet that wanted to go on strike. "Hey, anybody home?"

They didn't answer her, of course. They were deep

in secret projects; maybe they were plotting to over-throw the government.

So long as they do it quietly.

The back door banged open with the sound of a cannon and Michael came in, as if mounted on an elephant. "Hi, Mom, how was your day?"

"Good, how was yours?"

Michael shrugged, indicating she knew not what. "I'm going to play some football now," he added, indicating that nothing, but nothing, should stand in his way.

"Fine," she said. "Have fun. Trample on." She gave a flick of her hand, as if giving permission, which hadn't been asked for. She resumed staring into her coffee cup and regrouping her energy. If a strange man was waiting upstairs in bed for her, he'd simply have to amuse himself until she had the strength to climb the stairs.

Michael put on his shoulder pads and grabbed his helmet; he was feeling violent today, he was *moving*. In two strides he was in the upstairs hallway, but Elliott stood there, blocking his way.

"Michael—"

"How you doin', faker..." Michael pushed on past.

"I've got something really important to tell you."

"Yeah, what?"

"Remember the goblin?"

"Goblin? Hey, get outa the way—"

"Wait a second, Michael, this is serious. He came back."

"Elliott—" Michael had little or no use for his younger brother. Elliott was a sort of weasel with nasty little moves, like the ones he usually made in Parcheesi. "Back off."

"I'm gonna show him to you, but he belongs to me."

Michael hesitated. "Well, make it fast."

"Swear first. The most excellent promise you can make."

"Okay, okay, let me see. What is it, a skunk or something? Do you have it in your room? Mom'll kill you."

Elliott led Michael down the hall. "Take off your shoulder pads," he said as they entered the room. "You might scare him."

"Don't push it, Elliott."

Elliott led him over to the closet. "Close your eyes."

"Why?"

"Just do it, will you, Michael?"

Within the closet, the elderly being was reviewing everything he knew about communication devices, which he must somehow build. He heard the two cabbage-heads come into the room, but ignored their approach, more intent on searching his brain for transmitter blueprints. The closet door suddenly opened.

Elliott put his arm around him and nodded reassuringly. "Come on, meet my brother."

They stepped out, just as Gertie, home from nursery school, raced into the room. Seeing the monster, she screamed, as did the monster, and Michael, who'd just opened his eyes. The mingled voices pierced to the command center of the house, where Mary sat, trying to pull herself together.

"Oh, God..." She rose from the kitchen table. What savage ritual was her family enacting now? It sounded like they were pulling Gertie's pants down. In twenty years, Gertie'd be trying to recollect it, on a psychiatrist's couch.

Mary climbed the stairs, ready to take notes, which she'd give to Gertie when her analysis began.

She walked wearily down the hall toward Elliott's room. A full day's work at the office, followed by infant trauma in the home—just another of life's little challenges.

She paused a moment outside Elliott's door. At least the room would be neat.

She opened the door. Every object Elliott owned had been dumped on the floor. Mary looked at him. How, in the midst of this, could he have such an innocent expression on his face? "What happened in here?"

"In where?"

"Where? Look at this mess. How is this possible?"

"You mean my room?"

"This isn't a room, it's an accident. Did you hire a whirling dervish?"

Inside the closet, the old cosmologist huddled between Gertie and Michael. The little girl seemed ready to bite him; the boy's mouth was hanging open in a dumb gaze, and his enormously misshapen shoulders were taking up considerable room in the tiny closet. The guest from space hoped this present arrangement would not be permanent, as quarters were cramped enough.

He peered out through a crack in the louvered door, at the mother of the house, who was pointing at the debris he'd strewn around the room in his search for transmitter parts.

He tried to gauge the friendliness of the Earth woman. She wore no metal chains, did not appear armed, and was every bit as attractive as the Martian princess in the poster, though of course she too lacked the supreme beauty of the pearish lower silhouette, and had nothing to comment on in the way of long toes.

"Elliott, I heard Gertie scream. Were you and Michael violating her in some way?"

"Hey, Mom—"

"You mustn't do things like that, Elliott. It's costly in the end. About ninety dollars an hour, to be exact."

"Mom, I didn't do anything."

"Then why was she screaming?"

"I don't know, she just came in, screamed, and ran back out."

Mary pondered this. Had she, as a little girl, run into rooms, screamed for no reason, and run back out? She had, frequently. And she felt like screaming now. Come to think of it, she'd just *been* screaming. Maybe she'd scream at Elliott a little more and then leave.

"I'm sorry, Mom."

"I didn't mean to scream at you, Elliott. I'm sorry too. But clean up your room or I'll kill you."

"Okay, Mom, you bet."

Mary turned and left the room. When her footsteps were sounding on the stairs, the closet door opened and Michael, Gertie, and the old monster came out.

Michael had changed profoundly in a few moments' time; he felt he'd been blocked on the fifty-yard line by a steam roller; his body was numb and he kept thinking he was dreaming, that maybe he *had* gone to football practice, had knocked heads with someone, and was unconscious. But there was Gertie, her regular annoying self; and there was rotten Elliott, life-size. And there was the monster.

"Elliott, we've got to tell Mom."

"We can't, Michael. She'll want to do the right thing. You know what that means, don't you?" Elliott pointed at the elderly voyager. "He'll wind up as dog food."

Harvey thumped his tail.

"Does he talk?"

"No."

"Well, what is he doing here?"

"I don't know."

The two boys looked at their five-year-old sister, who was staring at the creature, her eyes wide.

"Gertie, he won't hurt you. You can touch him."

The stranded old traveler submitted to more probing and prodding, the children's fingertips pulsing their messages inward to his deep receptors, and though the messages were chaotic and confused, these little coconuts weren't stupid. But could they lift him into the Great Nebula?

"You're not going to tell, are you, Gertie? Not even Mom?"

"Why not?"

"Because—grownups can't see him. Only kids see him."

"I don't believe you."

Elliott took Gertie's doll from her hands. "You know what will happen if you tell?" He wrenched the doll's arm up behind her back.

"Stop it! Stop!"

"Promise not to tell?"

"Is he from the moon?"

"Yeah, he's from the moon..."

Mary lay on the bedroom floor, exercising along with the TV. The show's hosts were a Swedish woman of fifty without a wrinkle, and her boyfriend, a low-grade moron who made his stomach muscles perform vaguely pornographic movements.

"...and one...two...three..."

Mary struggled to follow them, got mixed up, turned off the sound, and just lay there on the rug in her favorite pose, the one in which she looked like she'd been shot in the belly with an arrow.

Faintly, from Elliott's room, she heard the voices of her three children. She knew they were hatching some scheme; there was a peculiar tension in the air.

Was that why her head was buzzing again? Or was it from the bizarre sexual-rejuvenation exercise she'd just tried to perform, with her ankle behind her ear? God, she'd never try that one again; her thigh muscle was still quivering, and not with passion.

She looked at the moron on the TV, who was silently mouthing instructions to her. Despite his low IQ, she had a crush on him and fantasized jumping hand in hand with him into the televised swimming pool, while the Swedish woman rotated her big toe with two fingers.

Enough, enough . . .

She switched off the tube. It was time to feed the mouths of hungry babes. "All right," she called, entering the hallway, "come and help me fix the dinner."

Naturally there was no response, and she proceeded on down the stairs alone.

Tonight we'll have turkey-gristle pot pies and—let me see—instant mashed potatoes would be a charming side dish, along with a handful of pretzels.

She labored over these preparations, her eyes occasionally going to the kitchen window, and the yard next door, where her neighbor was riding his lawn-mower like a demented giant on a kiddy-mobile. Her own yard had no grass, of course, because of Harvey, who insisted on digging it up in search of nonexistent bones. He looked at her now, ears begging in that way he had, one up, one down. "Who ate the broomstick, Harvey? Anyone we know?"

Harvey licked his chops, his tongue going up over his nose.

"Why, Harvey? What did you see that excited you? Did that little French poodle go by again with the bow in her curls? Is that what set you off?"

Harvey nodded, growling low, then whimpering. Food had not been forthcoming all day. Everyone had forgotten the main business around here, of feeding dogs. What was going on? Was it because of the monster upstairs?

I will have to eat him, thought Harvey, quietly.

Mary went to the stairs and graciously announced dinner: "Come down or else!"

Eventually there was the patter of rhinoceros-steps on the stairs, and her brood appeared, looking secretive.

"What're you up to? Come on, I can read you like a book."

"Nothing, Mom." Michael sat down, Gertie beside him.

Gertie looked at the pot pie. "Yuck."

"Shut up, dear. Elliott, please pass the salt."

"I made a house in the big closet today." Elliott looked shiftily at her.

"What kind of house?"

"Sort of like a hideout."

"Oh, really, how did you find the time with all the messing up you had to do?"

"Can I keep it?"

"You're not using it to escape from responsibility, are you, Elliott? Young boys should not spend all their time in a closet."

"Not all the time. Just some of the time."

"I'll give it careful consideration," said Mary, by which they all knew she had no choice, that Elliott would torment her about it until she capitulated. She tried to change the subject, gracefully. "Aren't these potatoes delicious?"

"Yuck."

"Do have some more, Gertie, since you like them so much."

"I eat better at nursery school," said Gertie. "We have big chocolate doughnuts."

"Really? I must talk to the head of the nursery school about that."

"He's a pervert."

"Gertie, don't use words you don't understand."

". . . a pervert, a pervert . . ." sang Gertie, quietly, over her potatoes, while Mary put her head in her hands.

Upstairs, the ancient fugitive crept out of the closet. The room was before him—a pile of clutter he'd created in his search for transmitter parts, a search he continued now.

His eyes swept the room, fine-focus on. The electrons of the room appeared, dancing their circular dance; but the inner cosmic whirl was of no help. He needed solid objects, such as—the record player.

He clicked his focus back to ordinary vision and shuffled over to the machine. The turntable was empty. He put his finger on it and gave it a spin.

How does a fork combine with this?

Answer to come, *over* . . .

He nodded. Escape was to be through spun signals, spun out into the night, threads of hope, hundreds of millions of them, radiant as the willow-creature's silken hair.

From below in the house came the sound of forks — he knew it well now—and of glasses, plates, and a distorted jabber that played in his ears.

"Mama, why do kids see things you can't see?"

"What have you been seeing, Gertie? Elliott's goblin?"

"Mama, what are the people who aren't people?"

The person who wasn't a person sensed that the children would not purposely betray him, but the little girl could be trouble, for she had no understanding of the need for secrecy.

However, for now all seemed secure. Dinner was finishing, a great quantity of M&Ms apparently having been consumed. He hoped they would bring him some soon.

"All right, who's doing the dishes?"

The willow-creature's voice came to him, along with her telepathic image, head crowned in waves of radiant fibers, finer than silk. If only her nose . . .

. . . were more like a bashed-in Brussels sprout . . .

He spun the turntable again with his finger.

Elliott's footsteps sounded on the stair, and then the boy entered the room, carrying a tray.

"Here's your supper," he said in a whisper, and handed it over.

On the plate were some lettuce leaves, an apple,

and an orange. The ancient student of plant life took the orange and ate it, peel and all.

"That the way you always do it?"

The elderly voyager frowned; his inner-system analyzer was advising him to wash it first, next time.

"How're you making out? You feel okay?" Elliott noticed the still-spinning turntable. "You want to hear something?"

The monster signaled that he did. Elliott put a record on and lowered the needle.

> *"Accidents will happen,*
> *but it's only rock 'n' roll . . ."*

The old star-tracker listened to the peculiar sound, and watched the black disc spin, his mind engrossed by thoughts of his transmitter. The Ship of Wondrous Night would not respond to rocks rolling down a hillside. He must send in the true speech of his people. How could he modify this sound? How could he multiply its frequency into the microwave region?

His ear picked up the voice of the willow-creature, down the hall.

"Gertie, what you doing, sweetie?"

"I'm going to play in Elliott's room."

"Don't let him torture you."

The child entered, pulling a little wagon filled with toys. In it she had placed a potted geranium, which she set at the old botanist's feet.

He stared down at the offering. His heart-light fluttered.

Thank you, little girl, that is very nice of you.

Harvey the dog entered. He sniffed the monster, and proceeded to the geranium. Did it need watering?

"Harvey, be cool."

Michael entered, hoping that somehow the monster would have vanished, but it was there and he had to deal with it. He studied it for a moment, then turned to Elliott. "Maybe he's just some animal that wasn't supposed to live."

"Don't be lame, Michael."

"But I don't *believe* in stuff like this..."

"I do, now. I always did, really."

Gertie was emptying her other gifts in front of the monster. "Here's some clay. Do you ever play with that?"

The extraterrestrial took it into his hand and lifted it to his mouth, preparing to bite off a sizable portion.

"No, silly, you *roll* it..." Gertie showed him how, and he proceeded to roll a ball in his palms.

"I have an idea," said Elliott. "Where's the globe?"

Michael handed it to him. Elliott turned it in front of the star-wanderer, to North America. "Look, see, this is where we are..."

The wanderer nodded, recognizing terrain he'd often seen, coming in at an angle like this above the planet in the Ship of Ages. Yes, he knew the planet, too well...

"Yeah," said Elliott, "that's where we're from. Where are you from?"

The old voyager turned, staring out the window at the star-filled sky.

Elliott opened an atlas and pointed to a picture of the solar system. "Are you from our part of the universe?"

The monster separated the modeling clay and laid five balls down on the map of the system, around a central sun-ball.

"Five? Are you from Jupiter?"

He could not understand their questioning jabber. He pointed at the five balls, and released an electron elevator from his fingertips. The balls rose up in the air and floated above the children's heads.

The balls orbited there, round and round, as the children groaned, the strength seeming to have gone out of their legs.

"Oh . . . no . . ."

Had he offended them?

He switched off the electron blanket and the balls fell to the floor.

Then he retired into the closet with his geranium.

"Mommy," said Gertie, "Elliott has a monster in his closet."

"That's nice, dear . . ." Mary had her feet up on the living room sofa and was doing her best not to listen to the children, something made more difficult now that Elliott had just swatted Gertie with a rolled newspaper.

"*Waaaaaaaaaaaa!*" screamed Gertie. "I hate you, Elliott."

"Stop this!" Mary turned within her layer of facial cream, her face feeling like it was submerged in axle grease, beneath which wrinkles were miraculously vanishing, she hoped. "Elliott, be nice to Gertie."

"Why?"

"Because she's your sister."

"Come on, Gertie," said Elliott, in a sudden change of mood, "I'll play in the backyard with you."

"That's better," said Mary, and rotated her head back on the sofa pillows. She stared out through her halo of cream, feeling as if she'd been hit in the face with a pie. But when she scraped it off, the New Me would emerge. *If* the house remained relatively quiet. She listened to Elliott guiding Gertie out through the back door. He could be so loving and gentle with her when he wanted to . . .

"If you say one more word about the monster," whispered Elliott as they stepped into the yard, *"I'll pull all the hair off your dolls."*

"You just try it," said Gertie, little fists balled on her little hips.

"Gertie, the monster is . . . a great gift to us." Elliott struggled with his thoughts, trying to voice this thing he felt, that some high purpose had come into their lives, that it was the best thing that had ever happened to them. "We've got to help him."

"Well, he looks like just a big toy to me," said Gertie.

"He's not a toy. He's a wonderful creature from *there*." He pointed to the sky.

"He still looks like a toy," pouted Gertie. "And Mommy said we should *share* our toys."

"I'll share him with you. But you've got to keep him a secret."

"A secret, a secret," sang Gertie, *"I know a little secret . . ."* She looked at Elliott, impish power in her

eyes. "What'll you give me if I don't tell?"

"What do you want?"

"Your walkie-talkies." Gertie smiled triumphantly. This *was* the best thing that had ever happened, getting her big brother to give in.

"Okay," he said, "you can have them."

"And you have to play dolls with me."

A pained look came into Elliott's eyes.

". . . so all the dollies are having tea. . ." Gertie was in her room, setting the play table. The various dolls were sitting around it, chatting nicely. ". . . and my doll says to your doll, 'Aren't boys horrid?' And your doll says. . ."

Elliott listened to what his doll had to say, and then he said it, making the doll's head move, making her hand reach out for tea. He recalled with fading happiness the times he used to roller-skate through Gertie's tea parties, knocking over dolls, chairs, table, and then roll away, laughing. Were those wonderful moments gone forever?

Mary passed their doorway and looked in. "Why, Elliott, how sweet of you."

"Elliott's going to play dolls with me *every night,*" said Gertie happily.

Elliott's dolly groaned and slipped under the table.

When Tyler arrived for Dungeons & Dragons, he was greeted by the strange spectacle of Elliott in the kitchen with Gertie, slaving over her little Betty Crocker play stove. Elliott was wearing an apron and had a tiny muffin tin in his hand.

"Hey, you crackin' up?" Tyler leaned his lanky, prematurely tall frame against the edge of the door. He was all legs and arms, and Elliott took this opportunity to call him Plastic Man, a name Tyler was sensitive about, conveying as it did his worst fear, that he might grow up to be seven feet tall.

"Whataya makin', Elliott?" Tyler hunched over the little stove, where Gertie was puttering in ecstasy, her enslaved brother mixing up some dirt and water. "Looks like a hash brownie."

"Get lost, will you, Tyler?" Elliott wiped his hands on the flowered apron.

"Yeah, well, we've got a D&D game on for tonight, remember?"

"He's playing with me," said Gertie, "for the rest of his life."

The back door opened and Greg the Ork entered, in his dayglo shirt that made him look like a melting neon Popsicle, an impression heightened by the fact that he drooled when speaking. "Hey, what's goin' on here?"

"Nothing, Dribble Lips," hissed Elliott from his muffin mix.

"Elliott and I," sang Gertie, "are making dragon pies."

Greg swung a chair around and sat on it, smiling crookedly, saliva spraying as he spoke. "Whadja, abuse her or somethin'?"

"Low, Greg," said Tyler, "very low."

Greg dribbled on the back of the chair. "I've seen everything now." He stared at Elliott, who, so far as he knew, had been like every other brother in the world, taking pleasure in playing with his sister only when the game was interesting—for example, tickling her until she nearly had a nervous breakdown, a game he often enjoyed with his own sister. Or tying her to a tree and *then* tickling her. Or crashing into the bathroom with four or five other guys while she was taking a bath, and then standing around laughing while she screamed. *Those* were the right games. But this? Thoughtful drops of spittle ran off Greg's lower lip, onto his neon shirt.

The last member of the Dungeons & Dragons team showed at the kitchen window: Steve, wearing a baseball hat with fat, floppy wings sticking out from it. He put his fingers behind the wings and wiggled them. Following this debonair greeting, he entered.

"Don't say anything," snarled Elliott, as he slipped his muffins in the little oven.

"What can I say?" Steve wiggled his hat-wings again. "These things happen." His own sister had blackmailed him. You had to be on your guard, keep doors locked, lights off. You had to be *cautious*.

"Elliott and I run a little bake shop," said Gertie, singing over her filthy pastries. "And everybody buys our cookies, even Santa Claus." She turned the knobs on the oven and closed the door. Then she looked at Elliott and let her impish secret play in her eyes, about the monster upstairs. Elliott winced and started another batch of muck muffins.

In the night, the extraterrestrial looked up from his pillows to see Elliott climbing out the bedroom window, onto the tiled roof.

Where was the boy going?

The space traveler gazed from his own little window, as Elliott crossed the slanted roof and then scampered down the stairs leading from it to the garden. In another moment he was out of sight.

The old star-rover monitored the boy's path telepathically: Elliott was climbing into the hills beyond the house. Did he go to get food for his friend in the closet?

No, the boy was creeping onto the dread fire road, where all troubles begin.

The extraterrestrial's delicate mind-antennae twitched spasmodically, for across the night he could feel—the clicking of teeth on the ring of terrible trophy.

Elliott was not alone on the fire road.

Another was there, searching in the shadows. Searching for whom?

Could there be any doubt?

He felt the heavy footsteps, felt the cold, staring eyes of the Earthman, a gaze that pierced the night with its own telepathy.

The aged space traveler switched off his mind-radar and huddled in the closet. They were after him, with their blinding lights. They were up there in the hills, covering every inch of it, their own mental radar telling them—the extraterrestrial is hereabouts, and we shall find him.

And stuff him.

Under glass.

He reached for an Oreo cookie and chewed it nervously. They must never find him. But they were so near. And Elliott was up there, spying on them. What if he was caught? Could he be made to reveal what he knew about a certain oddly shaped guest in his closet?

He turned toward his geranium and gave it a pleading glance. The plant turned on its stem, faced him. Its tight buds unfolded and it bloomed all at once in a burst of brilliant red flowers.

Then it sighed, nearly expiring from the tremendous effort, but the space-botanist stroked it with his long fingertip and murmured softly. His cosmic speech, the quintessence of experience on innumerable worlds, renewed the plant, and stabilized it in its glorious blossoming.

Your voice is purest gro-formula, Ancient Master, said the geranium.

Yes, but it isn't English.

The aged voyager scratched his head. English was what he needed, in order to get about better and make his wishes known.

Gertie had brought him her ABC book. He took it in his lap and slowly traced the letters M... and... M.

Elliott lay in the brush by the side of the fire road and watched the government agents pass, their lights sweeping in all directions. If they spotted him, he'd just say he was out walking his dog.

Harvey crouched beside him, shivering nervously. The animal had an uncontrollable urge to rush out and bite the man with the keys. Anyone with that many keys, Harvey felt, *should* be bitten.

"There's nothing here tonight," said one of the agents.

"I know. But I still have the feeling we're being watched." The man with the keys swept his light along the edge of the road. "But by whom?"

By a half-starved dog, said Harvey to himself, and wondered if emergency Milk-Bone rations might be present in one of the vehicles parked on the fire road.

He tried to edge forward, but Elliott held him down.

"Cool it, Harvey..." whispered Elliott, and backed off into the deeper shadows. In another minute he was sliding silently down the sandy hillside, Harvey rolling along beside him.

The night was lit with a billion stars, and Elliott knew he had one of the great secrets of the night, hidden in his room. He would never sell that secret, never surrender it, not even if they caught him and tortured him.

Harvey, for his part, would sell out for a single Milk-Bone, but nobody was asking him. He pawed along, trying to formulate a plan.

"Harvey," said Elliott quietly, "we have a great treasure with us. Do you know that?"

Harvey stared down at the passing sidewalk. All he knew was that there wasn't enough dog food in the world.

"I love him, Harvey. He's the best little guy I ever met." Elliott looked up at the stars and tried to imagine which one belonged to his new friend.

They all belong to him, said a whisper from the moonlight.

Harvey's ears perked up.

Did I hear someone? Rustling a bag of kibble?

He looked around, but the street was empty.

Mary woke to a noise on the roof. She removed her herbal eyepads and sat up.

But the sound had already ceased and the house

was still again. She went to the window and looked out. The garden was empty, except for Harvey, who was furiously digging a hole.

She drew the shade on the demented dog, and returned to her bed. Something strange was going on, she knew it. But what? What were her children up to?

She smoothed out her pillow and embraced it sleepily. The dream she'd been having returned to her. She'd been dancing, how nice . . .

. . . with someone who only came up to her navel.

Her eyelids fell; the strange music began again—an odd, alien sound, with squiggles and bleeps—and she felt herself going around once more, her partner out of sight below, nose pressed to her stomach.

"We've got to tell, Elliott. It's too serious."

"No, he wants to stay with us."

The two brothers were walking toward the school-bus stop. Michael was upset. His world had been turned upside down. Weird ideas kept moving through his head, about satellite paths and the surface of Mercury, instead of end runs and quarterback-sneaks, the important things in life. "He's a man from outer space, Elliott. We don't know what he's gonna do or why he's here. We could wake up and all be on Mars or something, surrounded by millions of these squashy guys."

Elliott wasn't listening; a new figure on the morning street had caught his eye. "That's not our regular milkman, is it?"

"He must be on vacation, that's some other guy."

"Michael, listen, there are people in this neighborhood, people who've never been here before. Look at that car up there, with a man sitting in it, reading a newspaper. They're *looking* for him."

"They? Who are they?"

"They're all around. They're up in the hills."

"You'd better figure something out pretty soon, Elliott, before they close in on us."

"He needs time to plan his strategy."

"Maybe he's not that smart, maybe he's like a worker bee who only knows how to push buttons or something."

"Michael, he's—he's so far ahead of us, you can't imagine."

"Yeah, then why is he living in our closet?"

"He had bad luck. But we're gonna change it."

"Elliott, you and I are just a pair of dumb kids, can't you understand that? If anybody helps him, it should be trained scientists or something. Guys with—with smarts. They could test him, feed him better."

"We're feeding him okay."

"Oreo cookies, Elliott. What kind of diet is that? Maybe you're killing him and don't know it."

Elliott's face grew tense, his voice strained. "Michael, if we turn him over to anybody else, he'll *never* get back to his home. I know that for sure."

"How, Elliott? How do you know?"

"I feel it, like it was burned into me. It comes to me over and over. That he chose us 'cause we're the only ones who could help him."

"But why us? We're nobody. We don't have any money, we don't have any ideas. We don't even have a father."

"None of that matters. He knows. We're the ones to—to put it together for him."

"Put what together?"

"Something. Something . . ." Elliott fumbled, as if he were just waking up from a dream he should remember but couldn't, a dream the space creature had sent him, a picture of what he needed. But the picture had already faded, and the bus stop was just ahead.

Tyler, Steve, and Greg were there, needling each other as they waited, and needling Elliott as he approached. "Hey, Elliott, how's the bake shop today? Make any fruit pies?"

"Kiss off, Tyler."

Greg sprayed Elliott with some advice about Gertie, spittle shining on his habitually twisted lip. It was thoughtful, sound advice. "Stuff her in the clothes hamper."

Steve wiggled his wings. "Say, Elliott, I forgot to ask—what ever happened to your goblin? Did he come back?"

The strain of Gertie's dolly games, of playing jacks and potsy, of baking an endless variety of topsoil tarts, had taken its toll on Elliott's spirit. He blurted out, "Yeah, he came back. And he wasn't a goblin. He was a spaceman."

"What, who's a spaceman?" A small red-haired boy pushed forward, speaking in a loud, nasal voice.

"You know how long it takes to get from Earth to Uranus?"

"Up *your* anus, Lance," said Elliott, already regretting his slip. Lance's ratlike gaze was bright, and he seemed to sense that something important was up.

The school bus pulled in to the curb and the boys climbed on, past a new driver. "Hey, what happened to George?"

"He's sick," said the new driver, whom none of the children had seen before.

Gertie had no nursery school today. She was supposed to, but she'd pretended to be sick and gotten the janitor to drive her home, where she could play in peace with the monster.

Because Elliott was keeping the monster all to himself.

She got out her wagon and started putting toys in it, which she knew the monster would like. She hoped he would stay with them forever and marry Mommy.

She pulled the wagon down the hall into Elliott's room, opened the closet door, and went in. The monster looked up and rolled his eyes. Gertie rolled her eyes, giggling, and sat down beside him, with her wagon. "Are you a big toy?" She looked him up and down. "Well, if you're not a big toy, what are you?"

He backed into the corner of the closet and seemed kind of scared. She wasn't scared at all, not anymore, because last night she dreamt the monster had taken her to a beautiful place far away in the stars. He'd

• 98 •

taken her hand and shown her wonderful flowers, and strange little birds had landed on his head, singing to him, and there'd been lovely light all around.

Now she took his hand. "Don't be scared," she said. "It's just like in the dream." She stroked his hand, petting it the way she petted Harvey. "Elliott and I are taking care of you, so you don't have anything to worry about, even if you are a great big toy. Here are all my dolls in the wagon, see? Don't they have nice hair? You don't have any hair, do you know that?"

The extraterrestrial gazed at the chattering child, and though she was better company than Harvey, how could such children really ever help him to reach his people? They could hide him, yes, for a while. But he needed high technology, not a wagonful of dolls.

"...and here's my rolling pin and this is my cowgirl vest, isn't it pretty? And this is my Speak and Spell. Did you ever play with one of these?"

The elderly alien took the bright rectangular box into his long fingers. His mind leapt suddenly into higher focus, and his heart-light fluttered.

"It teaches you to spell," said Gertie. "See..."

She pressed a button on the box, a button marked *A*. The Speak and Spell spoke to Gertie. It said, quite clearly, in a man's voice, *"A..."*

She pressed the *B* button and it said, *"B..."*

The old voyager pressed the *M* button and heard, *"M..."*

"Now you watch this," said Gertie, and pressed a button marked *Go*.

The box spoke. *"Spell 'mechanic.'"*

Gertie pressed buttons, but her spelling wasn't all that good yet. The box said, *"No. Wrong. Try again."*

She tried again. The box said, *"That is incorrect. The correct spelling is M-E-C-H-A-N-I-C."*

The space-being stared at the instrument, eyes flashing. Yes, it would teach him to speak an Earth language. But more important, far more important—in fact, the most important thing of all things in the universe at that moment—it was a computer.

His mind-scan was already inside it, racing over the microprocessor, the speech synthesizer, the memory chips.

"Hey, you okay?" Gertie touched the ancient creature, whose hands were trembling.

He nodded at the child, but his gaze remained fixed on the precious instrument, while his brain raced, sending solutions, alternate solutions, paths and by-paths to freedom—all of them born from this little box.

Gertie pressed buttons again.

"Spell 'nuisance,'" said the box.

She engaged in some incorrect spelling, and the senior scientist watched her play, and waited until she grew tired.

"Well, Mr. Monster, that's your spelling lesson for today. I'll be back."

The child skipped out. The monster flipped the box over in his lap, and removed its back.

Wonder of wonders...

He caressed the circuits.

Here was the heart of his transmitter.

He munched an Oreo and began. A radiant schematic of the Speak and Spell appeared in his mind as he gazed, its secrets becoming his own. Stored information, and the methods of storage, were child's play to an old space-hound like himself. Computers were familiar friends. Fancy finding one that spoke!

"Spell 'mechanic' . . ."

His ear-flap opened and he listened intently to the machine, his mind quickly grasping the phonemes on which the language was built.

"Spell 'nuisance' . . ."

His own circuits buzzed, assimilating, synthesizing. A glaze came over his eyes as his mind shifted into higher learning bands. On other planets—dead planets, lost planets—he had studied the tablets of ancient tongues, eventually mastering them. Here in his lap, now, was such a tablet—the Speak and Spell of Earth, the electronic stone by which he could master the signs and sounds of this planet.

"Spell 'refrigerator' . . ."

The subtle radiance of the word appeared on his inner scan, and he saw the object mentioned, saw a refrigerator, the place where milk and cookies were kept.

"Re-frigg-errr-a-tor . . ." His mouth wrapped itself around the word and the concept, simultaneously. His stomach seemed to speak and understand too, all his inner coordinates firing around this precious sound.

Thus inspired, the language center of his marvelous brain came fully on, a thousand stored tongues reappearing, as reference and cross-reference took place, so that Earth's language could be viewed in the round. He grasped its fundamentals, and then its delicate edges.

"Can-dy . . . cake . . ."

Soon he would have a complete working vocabulary, one that would allow him to function anywhere in society, and say the important things.

"Ice . . . cream . . ."

He pressed the machine's button, again and again. Truly, it was a friendly device, both teacher and companion. But it was more than that.

For, speaking Earth language already, this machine with a computer inside it could be made to speak yet another language. It would be his own language, and he would broadcast it to the stars.

His only error of the day was remaining in standby telepathy with Elliott. His full attention being on the Speak and Spell, he forgot about Elliott, but fine telepathic connections remained, and they gave Elliott a very difficult time, for Elliott was supposed to be cutting up a frog in biology class.

The teacher was about to begin. But one of his students was receiving an incandescent message, concerning the schematic of a Speak and Spell.

"We're going to peel back the skin . . ." The teacher pointed to the tub of live frogs. ". . . and take a look inside." He picked up one of the frogs and made a red line down its belly. "We'll make our incision line—Elliott, just what do you think you're doing?"

The teacher stared down at Elliott's lab report, which Elliott was furiously covering with diagrams of highly sophisticated electronic circuitry, his hand moving as if it were writing automatically, as if controlled by a ghost.

The ghost, of course, was the extraterrestrial in Elliott's closet, his mind overriding Elliott's with the mysteries of digitized speech and programmable memory.

But the teacher didn't know this. His student, always something of a problem, was ignoring the lesson completely, was writing so feverishly that his brow was covered with sweat, and everyone in the room was suddenly watching him.

"Elliott—"

The boy wrote, right off the edge of the paper, onto the desk. His arm wrote in the air. He walked to the front of the room, snapped up the frog anatomy chart, and began writing in chalk on the blackboard.

Tyler, Greg, and Steve stared in amazement. Tyler stretched his long legs out under the biology bench and tapped Greg on the ankle. Then he pointed at Elliott and made a whirling screw-loose sign with his finger near his head.

Greg nodded, copious amounts of excited saliva collecting at the corner of his mouth, as he watched Elliott scribbling like a maniac on the board, weird diagrams flowing from his chalk like the insides of a radio or something. A nervous bubble formed on Greg's lip; it was to blow such bubbles that he saved saliva. He had never succeeded in actually getting a bubble to float off his lip into the air, they always broke when he tried to blow them away, but a perfect specimen suddenly launched itself and sailed off toward the teacher, breaking on the back of his head.

The teacher didn't notice; he was screaming at Elliott. "Young man, sit down at once!"

He grabbed Elliott's arm, but it was infused with a power far beyond that of a boy; it felt like a pulsating rod of iron—and its cryptic creation was quickly covering the board and creating pandemonium in the classroom.

"Class dismissed! We'll continue this next week. Elliott!"

The chalk snapped in Elliott's finger and fell to the floor. He turned toward the teacher, his eyes fogged, mind carrying the combined expertise of a corporation's full computer staff, all of it having descended on him at once, out of nowhere.

". . . analog to digital . . ." he muttered, and the teacher yanked him into the hall, a tiny drop of blood at the end of Elliott's nose.

Steve took his winged hat out of his pocket and put it on; he fluffed out the wings and shook his head, as he watched Elliott being dragged toward the principal's office. "He'll be cleanin' erasers for a month."

"He's crackin' up," said Tyler.

"Maybe he found Mary's diet pills," said Greg. "Didn't she used to have some pretty good uppers?"

"Listen," said Steve, "this is because of all those mud pies he's been makin'. I know what a little sister can do to you." He smoothed back his wings. "She can wreck your life."

Gertie sat up from her coloring book and wondered why she was coloring at all, when she had the monster to play with. But something had moved her out of the closet and sent her down the hall into her own room. Now she had popped awake and wanted to play with the monster some more.

She walked back down the hall to Elliott's room and went in. As soon as she entered, she remembered more about the dream she'd had the night before: she and the monster had been off at the faraway place, sliding down a waterfall, hand in hand.

She opened the closet door. The monster was playing with her Speak and Spell. She looked into his big, funny eyes and she saw the dream-waterfall there, every color in the rainbow shining as the water danced.

The old traveler set the Speak and Spell aside. His mind was satisfied now, having swallowed whole the complicated circuitry, the best mental meal he'd eaten since he'd come to the planet.

But he'd completely forgotten the children, and he mustn't do that, for they were absolutely necessary. Without them, his work could not succeed. From the tiny hands of this child he'd received the all-powerful Speak and Spell. What other gifts had she in store for him?

"Come on, Monster. The coast is clear..."

Gertie led him by the hand, her fingers dwarfed in his immense palm, upon which was written the fate of a star-man—that three children of Earth would help him back to the stars. But the line of fate is the hardest of all to interpret, as he knew, and the creases crossing his were many, leading up—or down.

Gertie toddled along in front of him, across the room and into the hall. "Come on, you'll like this . . ."

He could nearly understand the child now, having spent his afternoon inside the reproduced wave-form of speech, in the Speak and Spell. Yes, it was time to try a little of this new language . . .

"Spell mechanic."

Gertie looked at him. "M-E-C-H-A-N-E-X . . ."

"That is incorrect."

"You know how to talk!" She dragged him along after her into her mother's bedroom, where the extraterrestrial picked up the full wave of the willow-creature. It was lovely at the center, but edged with loneliness.

Young willow-creature, Mexico is just a blip in the much greater screen—and there is a handsome admirer nearby . . .

Blip-blip . . .

He looked out the window and saw her, just pulling into the driveway and parking, near her vegetable garden. A kindred soul, after all, was she not? Loving vegetables as he himself did? Was this not the basis for a more extended, more intimate . . . relationship? Dare he show his eggplantish profile to her?

No, it seemed insane. She could not understand

his presence in her son's closet. It would be too difficult to explain, even in his new-found mastery of her language.

That is correct. Now spell nuisance.

"Mommy's in the garden," said Gertie. "She can't hear us here."

Gertie tiptoed over to the TV and turned it on. A prancing Muppet appeared, eyes boggling much in the fashion of the extraterrestrial.

He moved closer to the screen.

"Can you count to ten?" asked the bug-eyed Muppet.

"Yes," said Gertie.

"One . . ." said the Muppet.

"One," answered the monster.

"Two!" sang out Gertie, rushing ahead. "Twenty, thirty, forty, fufty!"

"Fufty," repeated the monster.

The Muppet danced upon his big feet. Gertie looked down at the intergalactical paddles on the space-being.

"Are you a Muppet?" she asked.

"No."

"Apple," said the Muppet.

"Apple," said Gertie.

The monster was edging toward the back of the TV, wishing to see its components more closely. His scanner was probing—the UHF tuner was what he needed, to multiply his Speak and Spell signal to the microwave frequency.

That is correct. Now spell beacon transmitter.

Here it was, he had only to remove it. However, it belonged to the willow-creature. He felt her attachment to it, to a certain program involving a man who flexed muscles and bounced around madly, an idiotic grin on his face.

Nonetheless, I must borrow it, temporarily.

Gertie, however, was playfully shrieking, and before the genial old scientist could remove the UHF tuner, she slapped a cowboy hat on his head, to match her own cowgirl's sombrero.

"Now we're both cowboys."

"B," said the Muppet.

"B," said the monster.

"I see by your outfit," sang Gertie, off key, "that you are a cowboy..."

"B. good," said the monster.

The high spirits of the shrieking child were sure to attract the mother. The old monster shuffled to the window and looked out. The garden was empty.

He pushed the cowboy hat out of his eyes and pointed to the hallway, toward his room. "Home."

"Say it again," said Gertie.

"Home."

Gertie shrieked with laughter.

The willow-creature's voice echoed from below. "Gertie, do you want to see the biggest pumpkin of your life?"

"I'm playing, Mommy. With the—with the—"

"B. good. B. good," said the monster.

He took her doll and twisted its arm. It acted like some sort of switch, he knew, to turn her off.

And at once she was quiet.

He led her quietly down the hallway, but then stopped to peek over the railing at the mother below, who was at the hall table, looking through mail.

Her gentle aura of rainbow light flowed out in every direction, and he lingered in the fringes of it, momentarily.

"Come on, monster," whispered Gertie.

She dragged him the rest of the way down the hall, into Elliott's trash-littered room. The closet door was open and Gertie pushed him inside, just as Elliott's voice came from downstairs.

"Hi, I'm home."

Gertie entered the closet with the monster. She picked up her Speak and Spell and pressed the letter *B*. What appeared on the display was a letter like none seen on earth before. And the voice that spoke from within the box no longer said the good old letter *B*. It said—*blip*.

Or something like that, something very strange in any case, and the old computer wizard smiled his great, turtlish smile.

"I wonder what's wrong with my Speak and Spell," said Gertie.

"Nothing," said the old being. His rearrangement of the signal was satisfactory; he'd broken the links in the chips and reprogrammed them with new vocabulary.

The closet door opened and Elliott entered.

"Elliott," said the monster from his pillows.

Elliott's mouth fell open.

"I taught him how to talk," said Gertie.

"You talked to me!" exclaimed Elliott. "Say it again."

"Elliott . . ."

"E.T. Can you say that? You're E.T."

"E.T.," said the extraterrestrial.

A knock came, three times on the door of the room. "That's Michael," said Elliott, and opened the closet. They stepped out into the room as Michael entered.

The monster looked at him. "Spell mechanic."

"M-E-C-H—*what?*"

Elliott smiled. "We taught him how to talk."

"*I* taught him," said Gertie.

Michael took one step closer. "What else can you say?"

"Spell nuisance."

"Is that all he can do? Tell you to spell things?"

The old wanderer shrugged modestly. He still couldn't understand the children very well, but he knew he could communicate the essentials. They would have to steal their mother's UHF tuner, while keeping him supplied with cookies.

The ringing telephone interrupted their talk, and Mary's voice floated up the steps. *"Elliott, it's for you."*

Elliott stepped into the hall, picked up the extension phone, and trailed it back into his room by its long cord.

"Hello, Elliott." Shrill, nasal tones filled the earpiece. *"This is Lance."* Elliott felt the dangerously inquisitive probe behind Lance's voice—Lance, who

never called him except to lie about how high his score had been in Asteroids; Lance, now suddenly talking about Saturn, and Mount Olympus on Mars, and other strange space things. *"... yes, Elliott, space, space, space. I seem to have it on the brain. Isn't that strange? Don't you feel something strange going on? I do..."*

"Hey, I gotta go..." Elliott hung up the phone and wiped his forehead. Lance was closing in, he could feel it.

So too could the telepathic old voyager, who'd monitored the call. The vibration was still inside him, of a too-curious child, of the kind that might—spell trouble.

And so, there was no time to lose. He pointed to the phone, and then to the window.

"Huh? Whattaya mean, E.T.?"

Again he pointed to the phone and the window, and the immensity of the sky. "Phone home."

"You want to—phone home?"

He nodded. "E.T. phone home."

"No, Elliott, calling your teacher a fruit is not a good enough answer."

"I don't know why he got so mad. I was just fooling around."

"What's come over you lately?"

"I'm okay, Mom. It's just a phase I'm going through."

"Please don't talk like a psychiatrist." Mary selected a dietetic cracker and crunched into its tasteless shape. It was mealtime, madness time, and if she gave into her real desires, she'd eat an entire loaf of buttered bread with raspberry jam, to soothe her nameless anxieties as well as those that had names, like Elliott.

"Do you ever meet monsters, Mommy?" asked Gertie.

"Frequently." What is more, thought Mary, I married one.

"I have a friend who's a monster," said Gertie, at which point Elliott picked up her doll and twisted its neck.

"Elliott!" screamed Gertie. "I'm sorry, I forgot..."

"Elliott, please," said Mary. "Don't be sadistic."

Gertie sniffled, and stroked her dolly. Elliott glared at her. Mary took a piece of bread, buttered it heavily, and glopped on several spoonfuls of jam. Moments later, with this in her stomach, she felt bloated and gross, so she had another slice, same style, to comfort her.

"Mom," said Michael, "you're eating your way through a loaf again."

"Shut up," said Mary softly, and tried to eat on, but Michael took the bread away, Gertie took the jam, and Elliott hid the butter.

She looked at them. "Thank you."

"The Mother Who Ate the World," said Michael.

"Right, right," said Mary, and plunged blindly toward the dishes, breaking the jelly-bread spell. "Don't let me near the stuff. Put it far, far away."

They did. They put it behind their backs, carried it upstairs, and fed it to E.T.

The inside of the Speak and Spell was exposed, its guts rewired, a few strands containing traces of raspberry jam. Instead of *mechanic, nuisance,* and other Earth words, the machine now said *doop-doople, skiggle,* and *zlock,* approximately, and much more no human ear could understand.

The boys sat beside him. He demonstrated, pressing the buttons.

"That's your language, E.T.?"

"E.T. phone home." He pointed out the window of the closet.

"And they'll come?"

He nodded.

But this was only part of his transmitter, this was only his message-maker. It must be set beneath the stars, and be made to run constantly, on and on, night and day, though no one be there to push its buttons. For this he needed a driving force, a thing to cause repetition, over and over.

He led them out of the closet, to the record player. By hand signs, half-sentences, and grunts he indicated his wish.

They stared, stupidly.

He pointed at the turntable and pantomimed putting down his own record.

They stared at him stupidly.

Frustrated, he paced back and forth, then spun around, opened his mouth, and tried to sing:

> *"It's onnn-leee
> rocks and roll-ing . . ."*

His voice, thought melodious in certain spheres of the universe, seemed to produce only snickers and giggles from the children. He glared at them. "E.T. make song."

They looked at him, still puzzled.

"Song, song, E.T. make song." He picked up a record and waved it around.

"You want to make your own record?"

"Yes, yes."

"Out of what?"

"Out of—out of—" He did not know out of what. He could only describe something round, a circular shape, which he made with his hand.

"You want something round?"

"Yes, yes."

"And you're gonna put a song on it?"

Michael stepped forward. "This isn't a recording studio. It takes a fortune to make a record."

E.T. pointed to his own head. "Spell mechanic."

"M-E-C-H—wait a second, whattaya mean? What does he mean, Elliott?"

Elliott looked at the monster. "You mean, you're a mechanic?"

"Yes, yes, spell mechanic." He turned the record player over and pulled out a handful of wire.

"Well," said Michael, "goodbye to that machine."

E.T. held up the wire. "More."

"You want more wire?"

He nodded.

"He wants more wire." They looked at each other, still wondering exactly how to humor their guest, but he was pacing the room on his paddle feet, intent on the higher solution.

To make his own rocks-and-rolling record he needed so much.

His mental whirlpool was showing him the device,

again and again, each time filling in another little piece. He needed . . .

. . . a coat.

He walked over to the closet, pulled out a coat, and put it on.

A fairly good fit, for one who had shoulders like a chicken, and of course, the button was a little tight over his great cannonball of a stomach. However . . .

He turned in it, wondering what in the name of the cosmic seas his dressing up in a coat had to do with a beacon transmitter.

No, you old flytrap, not the coat.

The coat *hanger*.

He stared at it, eyes clicking, brain whirring. The wooden coat hanger seemed to glow and swing, its shape hypnotizing him. He would bolt it to the record player, and then . . .

. . . spell *tracking-arm*.

He grabbed the coat hanger, pointed his finger at its dowel, and burned holes in it, one for every wire connection on the Speak and Spell.

"Hey, you've got a finger like a torch, E.T."

Still clad in his new coat, he hurried back into the closet, to his Speak and Spell. His torch-finger quietly melted the solder on the keyboard contacts, to which he fastened what wires he had. "More . . . more . . ."

The boys looked in the door. He waved the coat hanger.

"More . . . more . . ."

• • •

They brought him wire, a pie tin, a mirror, and a hubcap.

He kept the wire, rejected the other objects. They would not do for his rocks-and-rolling record. It must be hard, flat, round. Couldn't they understand?

He turned to his geranium.

They are Earth children, said the plant. Good, but slow.

"Okay, E.T., we'll find some other stuff."

"Yeah, there's lots of junk around..."

He watched them depart. He must not be impatient with them. He must be a M-E-C-H-A-N-I-C, soldering all the wires in place on the Speak and Spell and stretching them up to the dowel of the coat hanger, to the holes. Into these holes, contact fingers must go, small and metallic, with lots of spring in them.

He'd seen such metallic fingers around, somewhere in this house. Where was it?

The radiant waves of the willow-creature, mother of the crew, came to him. He closed his eyes and concentrated on her mental image, hovering before him.

Yes, she had the metallic fingers in her hair. What did she call them? He dipped into her memory chip, searched, found.

"Gertie..."

His other accomplice came running in. He pointed his finger at her. "Spell 'bobby pins.'"

"B-O-P-P-Y—"

"That is incorrect." He pointed at his slippery, hairless head.

"You want some?"

He nodded.

Gertie took him by the hand.

Together they snuck down the hall and into Mary's bedroom. He glanced out the window. The willow-creature was in her garden again, dealing with the largest vegetables in the state. A deeply puzzled atmosphere was about her head, as she hefted a gigantic squash, so big it appeared to have been milk-fed with a straw.

The potted flowers on the windowsill, radiant with out-of-season blossoms, bent to him.

Hello, Ancient Master. What are you looking for? What high, wonderful scientific mission are you on?

"Bobby pins."

"Here," said Gertie, opening up a white porcelain chicken.

The extraterrestrial took out the bobby pins, and caught his own reflection in Mary's dressing mirror. If he wore not only a jacket, but pants as well—would the willow-creature be able to overcome her shock?

He would have to shorten the pants and get paper bags for his feet. But then—

"Come on, E.T.," said Gertie, pulling at his hand. She pulled him out of the bedroom, into the hall. He followed her back to Elliott's room, and reentered his closet.

"What're you gonna do with Mommy's bobby pins?"

He sat down on his pillows and fastened the bobby pins to the dowel of the coat hanger. Now a row of metallic contacts hung down, to rake across the surface of his rocks-and-rolling record. He connected the pins to the wires leading from the Speak and Spell.

"That sure is a funny-lookin' thing," said Gertie. "Do you always make such funny things?"

"Yes."

"What for?"

"E.T. phone home."

"Where's your home?"

He pointed to the sky. Gertie stared out the little window.

"Is it where you take me when we go dreaming? The faraway place?"

"Far."

"Will they hear you at your home?"

Earth children asked an amazing number of questions.

"Will they pick up their phone and say, 'Hello, E.T.?'"

"Spell 'nuisance.'"

"N-U-S—"

"That is incorrect."

"Well, the reason I can't spell so good is you took my Speak and Spell, and now it only says gleeple deeple."

"Gleeple *doop*le."

"Anyway, it *doesn't* spell nuisance."

Gertie turned away from the monster and began playing with her stove, which she'd brought into the closet with her. She was baking a new kind of muffin made out of Mommy's face cream mixed with mud.

The elderly computer mechanic toiled on by himself, humming a confused smattering of Top-Forty lyrics he'd heard on Elliott's radio. So engrossed was he in his work, and Gertie in hers, that they didn't hear Mary climbing the stairs. They didn't hear her coming down the hall. They only heard her as she opened the door to Elliott's room.

The old monster jumped, lining himself up with the stuffed animals, goggling Muppets, and toy space robots in the closet doorway. His limbs froze in standby position, and his great interplanetary eyes, more evolved than Earth's greatest optical devices, went as dumb and unseeing as Kermit the Frog. Glazed, they stared out, and his lumpish form seemed lifeless as the toy robot to his right.

Mary entered. Her eyes flitted over the cluttered assortment of toys, met the extraterrestrial's gaze, and passed on to the geranium, flowering in the closet. "Did you bring this in here, Gertie?"

"The man in the moon likes flowers. He makes them grow."

Mary stroked the luxuriant foliage and shook her head in wonder. "Everything's growing like crazy. I can't understand it."

"Have a muffin, Mommy."

"My, this looks good," said Mary, looking into the muffin tin. Too good, she realized, for something made out of mud. The aroma was faintly familiar...

"My God, Gertie, is this my facial in here?"

"It's banana cream."

Mary stared at the remains of the secret formula

for the New Me. "Gertie, I'm not going to lose my temper, honey. I know you didn't know any better. But Mommy pays twenty-five dollars a jar for this cream and now I'll have to put it on my face mixed with mud, sand, and pebbles."

"I'm sorry, Mommy."

"I know you are, dear. And someday I'll laugh about it. But not today."

Her eyes passed back over the frozen extraterrestrial lined up with the Muppets, and she didn't so much as blink, so distraught was she over her defiled facial. She turned away and he breathed a sigh of relief, which was tinged with melancholy, however. For how could she love him when he was no more to her than Kermit the Frog?

He watched her leave the room, and his heart was heavy as he disengaged himself from the strings of a hanging puppet. He was just a toy to Mary, in the closet with the rest of the stuffed freaks.

Unhappy space-being, spell *loneliness*.

Spell *rejection*.

He squatted back down with his transmitter and soldered a few more wires with his torch-finger.

How ironic it was that the willow-creature, the lovely Mary, pined for her vanished husband while in a closet, close at hand, dwelt one of the finest minds in the cosmos. He gazed down at his large pumpkin stomach, hanging on the floor, and for the first time in his very long life he saw it as grotesque. But even if he stopped eating Oreo cookies, it would never go away. It was *him*.

"Why are you so sad, E.T.?" asked Gertie. She looked into his eyes and saw that the dancing waterfall had turned into a desert filled with big bare cracks that went on forever, the loneliest place she'd ever seen.

He blinked and the desert vanished. Then he picked up the Speak and Spell and touched the keys once more.

. . . gleeple doople zwak-zwak snafn olg mmnnnnip . . .

The soothing tones of higher intelligence comforted him. *That* was a language. You could speak your heart with it. He would speak to the night, over and over, as soon as the boys came back from shoplifting at the hardware store.

When he left the Earth, at least he'd have that satisfaction behind him, that he'd trained and guided these young Earthlings into the higher paths.

If he left the Earth.

Looking at his homemade transmitter, made of bobby pins and a coat hanger, he had his doubts. But his own inner brain wave assured him he was on the right track. He could only follow its directives and hope.

But if they hadn't stolen him a circular saw blade . . .

There was a clatter of footsteps on the stairs and then Elliott and Michael entered. They opened their jackets and took out the requested circular blade, as well as handfuls of eye bolts and other connectors.

"Here y'go, E.T. Is that what you wanted?"

"Spell rocks-and-rolling . . ." E.T.'s fingers moved

excitedly over the surface of the blade. He placed it on the turntable and spun it with his finger. The tooth-edged blade went round and round, glistening in the shaft of sunlight entering at the little window.

"But how can you make a record out of a saw blade?"

"Spell paint." He indicated that the surface must be coated.

"Any particular kind?"

He pointed at the sky.

"Blue?"

He nodded.

"Mommy came in," said Gertie. "And she didn't even notice E.T."

"Yeah? The camouflage worked?" Elliott pointed at the row of silly stuffed creatures.

"Out, out," said E.T. and chased them away. There was only so much humiliation a distinguished cosmologist could put up with in a day.

Mary gazed into the mirror over her dressing table and reached into the porcelain chicken for a bobby pin.

Her fingers moved around the empty interior of the bird.

"Where—?"

But she knew where. Gertie, of course. She was already using makeup. Bobby pins were necessary, as well.

"Gertie!"

The child came running in. "Yes, Mommy?"

"Give me back the bobby pins."

"I can't, the monster's using them."

"Oh? What is he using them for?"

"In his machine."

In his machine. Mary contemplated this. Was it worth the struggle of tracking through the child's endless string of fantasies to get the bobby pins back? No, clearly it wasn't. Better to let my own hair hang in my face, for that fashionable brink-of-a-nervous-breakdown look.

"Thank you, Gertie, that will be all for now."

"I'll tell the monster you said hello."

"Yes, give him my best."

The monster sat in his closet, working hard. The saw blade had been painted and allowed to dry, and now the senior mechanic began burning a pattern of holes in the painted surface.

"Hey," said Elliott, "I get it. It's gonna be like a music box."

Michael peered in over Elliott's shoulder as the pattern was inscribed. "It's a player piano," he said, as E.T.'s torch-finger continued burning a punch-card pattern in the blade. E.T. then laid the programmed blade on the turntable, gave it a spin with his finger, and lowered the coat-hanger arm; its row of bobby pins tracked along over the rotating blade, clicking in and out of the punched program.

"Wow, E.T., you're wild . . ."

As the blade turned and the bobby pins tracked, their wires activated the keyboard of the Speak and

Spell, and the star language came out, over and over.

. . . gleeple doople zwak-zwak snafn olg mmnnnnip . . .

"You made it, E.T. You made your own record."

Gertie came in, carrying her newly acquired walkie-talkie. She was talking to her distant dollies, in her own room. "Come in, dolly, this is Gertie . . ."

E.T.'s long arm reached out, took the walkie-talkie, and in two seconds he had dismantled its microphone and attached it to the Speak and Spell speaker.

"E.T., you wreck all my toys!" she shrieked, in tones that penetrated the entire house.

Her brothers patiently explained, while twisting the arms of her doll into hideous postures, that she must learn to be generous.

"Well," she sniffled, "he'd better not wreck anything else."

The aged scientist assured her that no more of her toys would be wrecked. All that was needed now was the coaxial cable from her mother's TV set. And the UHF tuner, for which the time had also arrived.

Together they snuck back down the hall.

Later that night, Mary entered her bedroom, clicked on the TV set, kicked off her shoes and got into bed. There, she wearily opened a newspaper and began to read. Eventually she noticed that the TV had not come on.

"Michael!"

The house was silent.

"Elliott . . ."

She pondered, her mother's intuition clearly telling her that her two boys were responsible. But this intuition, in a more refined burst, came up with the image of Gertie.

"Gertie?" she asked the night softly. Had Gertie done something?

She closed her eyes and a puzzled frown came across her brow, for she was getting a mental image of Gertie tiptoeing into the bedroom with a large Muppet.

I've been working too hard, sighed Mary, and stretched out with the newspaper over her face.

After a brief, anxious nap, she woke, hungry. Was it time to eat a loaf of bread smeared with strawberry jam? Had the Hour of Depravity come once more?

She slipped quietly from bed and tiptoed into the hall. The children mustn't see her; it was wrong to set them a bad example, of a mother who could not control her appetite, who at this very moment was beset by visions of jelly.

She paused in the hall, heard Elliott and Michael in the playroom. Good, they wouldn't see her making a disgusting pig of herself, but what was more important, they wouldn't stop her.

My thoughtful sons, who don't want me to have to squeeze sideways through the doorway of life.

But I can't help myself.

I'm starving.

For jelly rolls. Bowls of custard. Rice pudding. How about a banana split?

She tiptoed down the stairs and paused in the lower

hall, to see if the coast was clear.

The living room was empty. The dining nook was dark.

Mary tiptoed along toward the kitchen. Turning the corner, she saw a light burning, and the next moment discovered Gertie, sitting at the table with cookies and milk. What she did not see was E.T., on a stool beside the refrigerator. The poor little space-goblin was huddling there, unable to hide, and expecting the worst.

But Mary was talking to Gertie, and pointing at the two plates on the table. "Who is that plate for?" she asked, staring down hungrily at the cookies displayed on it. "For your doll?"

"For the spaceman," said Gertie. "He likes cookies."

"Would he mind if I had one?"

"Oh, no," said Gertie. "He loves you."

"What a nice spaceman," said Mary, and snatched up the cookies.

Oh, god, sugar.

The monstrous delight broke onto her taste buds, and she knew she was lost. "I must have jelly."

She whirled toward the refrigerator, threw it open. The door, swinging wide, knocked E.T. off his stool, into the trash basket. He sank to the bottom of it, feet sticking out, but Mary still did not see him.

"...apple butter...marmalade...how about these frozen blueberry turnovers, I could eat four of them..."

"Mommy," said Gertie, "are you having a fit again?"

"Yes, dear...fudge...an eclair..."

Suddenly, strong arms took her from behind.

"Control yourself, Mom."

"Elliott...Michael...leave me alone."

"Mom, please." Michael turned her from the spectacle before her. "You told us we were never to let you do this."

"Forget what I told you." She strained for the cookies on Gertie's plate.

"Come on, Mom," said Elliott, backing in front of E.T., whose feet were still sticking out of the trash basket. "We'll play Monopoly with you."

Mary looked into Elliott's eyes, could see he was anxious and nervous, hopping back and forth in front of her, to distract her from the refrigerator. "You're a loving child, Elliott."

"You told us to remind you," said Elliott, "that if you ate any more sweets, you'd look like a stuffed sausage in your bathing suit."

The two boys moved her away from the monster, out of the kitchen, and into the hall, Mary shuffling along between her sons.

"You're good boys...strict, but good..."

They got her moving upward again, on the stairs.

"Don't look back, Mom. You know what will happen if you do."

"The Hefty Ladies' Department," said Mary meekly, and continued on up the stairs.

On the following day it rained. Mary went to the umbrella stand for her umbrella. It wasn't there, and she didn't find it anywhere else, because it was in the closet upstairs being used as a parabolic reflector.

"Wow," said Elliott, "that's neat..."

The umbrella was lined with reflective foil. To its handle a coffee can was attached, with the UHF tuner, from which the coaxial cable ran back to Gertie's walkie-talkie mike; the mike was connected to the Speak and Spell, and *gleeple doople zwak-zwak* was now being multiplied into the microwave frequency. The ancient radio operator explained that he now needed something he'd spied under the dash of Mary's car.

"The Fuzz Buster? You want Mom's Fuzz Buster?" Michael shook his head, and Elliott agreed.

"That's the only thing of Dad's that Mom has left. She's very attached to it."

The elderly voyager made diagrams and showed the boys how the Fuzz Buster must be mounted in the coffee can so the microwave frequency could be transmitted outward.

And that evening, as Mary was speeding home, her warning system failed to show police radar in use, and she was given a twenty-five-dollar fine.

But the communicator was nearly complete.

"Yeah," said Michael, "but what's gonna run it? What's gonna turn *this?*" He spun the saw blade on the turntable. "If we take it up in the hills there"—he pointed out the window—"there won't be any electricity."

The space-being had just completed supper. Torch-fingering his butter knife, he took out the temper, then bent and bolted it to the coat hanger, along with the fork, to form a ratchet device: knife and fork moved in and out of the teeth of the sawblade, advancing it tooth by tooth.

"Yeah," said Michael, "but we can't stand out there all night, yanking that thing around."

The extraterrestrial continued smiling. He understood it all now, those early hints flashed at him from within, of a little fork dancing around a plate. It was this thing he'd made, and it would work, out in the hills, and no hands, human or otherwise, would be needed to activate it.

"So who's this?"

"My new character."

"What is he?"

"Magic-user, first level. Here's his chart."

"Let's hear it."

"Wisdom 20, Charisma 20, Intelligence 18, Strength 14."

"Name?"

"E.T."

E.T. could hear the Dungeons & Dragons game in the kitchen below, but he was much more interested in listening to something else that came about each night in the house, for which he needed only to press his ear against Gertie's door. He crouched low, bent his head forward, and continued to learn the history of Earth. Mary's voice came softly:

"Peter says, 'The redskins were defeated? Wendy and the boys captured by the pirates? I'll rescue her!

I'll rescue her! Tink rings out a warning cry. Oh, that is just my medicine. Poisoned? Who could have poisoned it? I promised Wendy to take it, and I will, as soon as I sharpen my dagger. Tink nobly swallows the draught as Peter's hand is reaching for it.'"

"Oh, no," said Gertie.

"Oh, no," whispered the old space voyager to himself.

"'Why, Tink, you have drunk my medicine! It was poisoned and you drank it to save my life! Tink, dear Tink, are you dying? Her light is growing faint, and if it goes out, that means she is dead! Her voice is so low I can scarcely tell what she is saying...'"

The elderly voyager lowered his head. This was indeed an awful thing.

"'...she says she thinks she could get well again if children believe in fairies! Do you believe in fairies? Say quick if you believe!'"

"I do," said Gertie.

"I do," said the ancient space traveler, tears forming in the corners of his eyes.

At which point Elliott came upstairs, looking for a Band-Aid, for he'd cut his finger on the cheese shredder. The age-old plant doctor turned, noticed the cut, and pointed his long finger at it. The tip of his finger glowed a brilliant pink. Elliott stepped back, startled by it, knowing that E.T. could burn holes in steel with that finger if he so desired. But E.T.'s finger only continued to glow warm pink, as he traced it across Elliott's cut. The bleeding stopped and the cut healed at once, as if it had never been.

Elliott stared down at it, astonished. He started to speak, to thank E.T., but the venerable doctor of the cosmos bade him be silent, and pressed his ear back to the door of Gertie's room.

"'If you believe in fairies, clap your hands...'"

The old traveler softly slapped his huge, unearthly palms together.

Then, deeper in the night, he stood at his little closet window and watched. The moon filled him with indescribable longing, and the Milky Way whispered its soft starlight into his heart. The radiances, material and subtle, all shone for his time-opened eyes; from the movement of the great stellar wheel he heard the hidden music of the stars and planets in flight, and felt their discourse in the darkness, the solemn voices of the giants reaching across the great distances.

He laid his forehead on the windowsill, mind and heart plunged in sadness. Once he had been part of the workings of the Great Wheel, had been allowed to witness the miracles of the universe, had seen the birth of a star. Now he stood in a four-by-five closet with a stolen umbrella and a stuffed Muppet.

He turned toward the creature, but the Muppet only stared glass-eyed at the night, lost in its own thoughts.

Cosmic loneliness invaded E.T.'s limbs. Every pore of his body ached with desire for starlight, up in the intimate range, where the beauty of Orion took one's breath away, glorious colors filling the nebula. And in the Pleiades, where the blue halo of a young star shines straight into the heart. And the Veil Nebula, drifting ever outward and whispering its majestic secret to those who drift with it in the sea of space.

Torn by these and other memories, he moved away from the window and slowly opened the closet door.

He tiptoed past Elliott's sleeping form, and entered the hallway. He moved silently down it, his misshapen shadow cast upon the wall, a walking squash, a strolling watermelon, a freakish figure in an alien land. His eyes were the eyes of Earth now—he had absorbed their ideas of beauty and form, and saw himself as truly grotesque, an outrage to eyes and mind, a cretin of impossible ugliness.

He peeked in Gertie's room, and watched for a few moments as the child slept. *She* thought he was attractive, but to her, Kermit the Frog was a dashing fellow.

He crept on down the hall to Mary's room, and peeked in.

The willow-creature was asleep, and he watched her for a long time. She was a goddess, the most beautiful thing he'd ever seen. Her radiant hair, spread out upon the pillow, was the moonlight itself; her fine features, so understated in their loveliness, were all that was perfection in nature—her closed eyes like the sleeping butterflies upon the night-blooming narcissus, her lips the petals of the columbine.

Mary, said his old heart.

Then, upon paddle feet, he tiptoed over to her bed and gazed more closely.

She was the loveliest creature in the universe, and what had he given her?

Nothing.

He'd stolen her Fuzz Buster.

He gazed on as she turned in sleep, dreaming whatever dreams she had, none of which, he knew, contained a potbellied old botanist from outer space.

Gently he placed an M&M on her pillow and crept back down the hall.

At the end of it, Harvey the dog was waiting.

Harvey's tongue hung out a bit as he stared at the strange being waddling toward him, like a bag of Gravy Train.

E.T. patted Harvey on the head. A current of *blip*s went down the dog's spine and made his tail curl up like a coat hook. He turned around, looked at it, looked at E.T.

Uncurl my tail, will you?

The space-being tapped the dog's nose, and the tail uncurled.

They continued on through the house, on their nightly prowl, something they did each evening after everyone else was asleep, Harvey padding along beside the houseguest, down the steps, to the rooms below. E.T. stopped in the alcove where the telephone was, and picked it up. He listened to its tone, then held the phone to Harvey's ear. The dog listened closely. He'd seen Elliott spin the dial of this thing with his finger and talk into it, and a little later, pizza showed up.

Harvey put his nose in the dial, turned it once, and hoped a steak sandwich would appear. E.T. added a few more spins of the dial, and then they listened to a sleepy voice answering.

"...hello?...hello?"

One steak sandwich, said Harvey, and a side order of Milk-Bones.

E.T. set the phone back into its cradle and they walked on, into the living room.

A color photograph of Mary rested on top of the TV set. E.T. picked it up and placed a kiss upon Mary's lips.

Then he showed the portrait to Harvey.

The dog, without sentiment, stared at the framed photo. The glass was smudged now, and since he got the blame for anything that was slobbered on around the house, he'd be nailed for this one too. He raised a paw and urged E.T. to replace the photo. But E.T. put it under his arm and carried it away with him.

So, thought Harvey, they'll think I ate it.

He regretted having eaten the bath mat, the broom, one of Mary's hats, and a pair of tasty leather gloves. Because it made people jump to conclusions.

E.T. prowled on through the living room. A vase of flowers stood on a table. He caressed them lovingly and murmured to them in his own tongue.

Harvey twitched his nose hopefully. In one of his doggie dreams he'd found a hamburger bush, and had been looking for it in the neighborhood ever since.

E.T. lowered a rose, into which Harvey eagerly buried his snout, but it was not a blossom from the hamburger bush, it was just a stupid flower.

E.T. tucked the flower tenderly against Mary's photo, entwining the stem into the filigreed frame, so that the rose and she were united—the two most beautiful things on Earth.

Then he continued on through the house, into the kitchen.

Harvey's tail began to wag, and his tongue circled once over his nose, for this room was the center of all a dog's hopes.

E.T. pointed. "Re-frigg-er-a-tor."

Harvey nodded enthusiastically, and a low whimper sounded in his throat. He'd tried for years to get his paw around the handle of this box, but evolution had denied him a thumb.

E.T. opened the box, took out milk and a Pepperidge Farm chocolate cake. Harvey whined pathetically, salivating, tail fanning the air, and E.T. presented him with a leftover pork chop.

Harvey fell upon it, joyful little growls in his throat as he tore at the tender meat. He paused momentarily to gaze up at E.T.

I'm *your* dog.

If any trouble comes around, let me know.

Upon the streets at nightfall, in addition to the Pizza Wagon, another van appeared, but it did not contain stacked boxes exuding the aroma of cheese and tomato. It was filled with audio-snooping devices sensitive enough to impress even an intergalactic traveler. And the operator at the illuminated control panel had a large ring of keys at his belt. Floating in upon him were voices familiar to us by now, the voices of the neighborhood:

"Mom, to make cookies, is a cup of milk the same as a cup of flour?"

And:

"Just get out of my life, will you?"

And:

"I'll be babysitting tonight, Jack, if you want to come over . . ."

The van moved slowly down the block, scrutinizing every voice, every conversation that took its place in the jigsaw puzzle of the neighborhood night.

"Peter says, 'The redskins were defeated? Wendy and the boys captured . . . ?' "

And:

"His communicator is finished, Michael. We can take it out and set it up . . ."

The man with the keys waved his hand and the van came to a stop.

"You know, Elliott, he's not looking too good lately."

"Don't say that, Michael. We're fine!"

"What's this 'we' stuff? You say 'we' all the time now."

"It's his telepathy. I'm—so close to him, I feel like I am him . . ."

To the ordinary snooper, this conversation would have been passed over as just a child's world of fantasy; to this particular snooper, it was as potent as a signal from Mars. The street map was brought out, and Mary's house marked with a large red circle. And the van moved off down the block, as the Pizza Wagon turned the corner . . .

Elliott explained Halloween to E.T. as best he could, pointing out that this would be E.T.'s only chance to walk around the neighborhood in plain view.

". . . because *everybody* will be looking weird. See? Hey, I'm sorry, E.T., I didn't mean that *you* were weird, just—different."

"Spell different," said E.T., as Elliott put a sheet over the old voyager's head, and huge, furry bedroom slippers over his paddles. The outfit was topped off by a cowboy hat.

"Looks good," said Elliott. "We could take you anywhere."

Elliott's own costume was that of a hunchbacked monster, to blend in with E.T. and make the space-goblin less unusual. Michael, downstairs with Mary, was having some difficulty with his costume.

"No," said Mary, "and that is final. You are not going as a terrorist."

"But all the guys are."

"You won't get four blocks in this neighborhood dressed like that."

"Please."

"No. And where's Gertie?"

"She's upstairs getting ready with Elliott."

But Gertie was not getting ready with Elliott. She was sneaking out a window.

Elliott turned to E.T. "Mom'll never know the difference, if you just keep quiet and shuffle along in your sheet. Okay? You're Gertie, got it?"

"Gertie," said the old monster, and shuffled along in his sheet, with Elliott, down the stairs.

Mary was waiting for them below. In an act of insane Halloween fervor, she'd gotten into a costume herself, wearing a leopard-pattern dress and an eye mask, as well as carrying a star wand with which to strike unruly trick-or-treaters on the head.

"Gee, Mom, you look great."

"Thank you, Elliott, that's very nice of you."

But not only Elliott was admiring her. The aged monster, disguised as Gertie and safely hidden inside a sheet, stared at Mary in wonder, for she looked like a star-creature, celestial, more beautiful than ever.

"Gertie," she said, stepping over to him, "that's a wonderful costume. How did you get your stomach so fat?"

She patted the great pumpkin shape, and the elderly voyager sighed faintly, to himself.

"We padded it with pillows," said Elliott nervously.

"Well, it's very effective," said Mary. "But let's put this cowboy hat at a more rakish angle."

Her hands came tenderly to the extraterrestrial's turtle-shaped head. Within the sheet his cheeks blushed as her fingers touched him. Delicious streams of energy flowed out of her, down his ostrich neck. His heart-light came on and he quickly covered it with his hand.

"There," said Mary, "that's better." She stepped back and spoke to Elliott. "Watch over her, and don't eat anything that isn't wrapped, and don't talk to strangers..."

Michael stepped into view, his terrorist costume modified. "...and don't eat any apples, 'cause they may have razor blades in them, and don't drink punch 'cause it may have LSD in it."

Mary leaned in, kissed both boys, and then kissed the space-goblin; his duckish knees buckled and his subcutaneous circuitry fluttered; lights as beautiful as Orion's nebula went off in his brain.

"All right," said Mary, "enjoy yourselves..."

Elliott had to drag the aged goblin off by the hand, for the creature was transfixed before Mary, as if looking at the birth of a star. He stumbled along in his bedroom slippers toward the door, but managed a last glance backward.

"So long, honey," said Mary.

So long, honey, he said silently, cosmic love-echoes resounding in his now-twisted brain.

They dragged him into the driveway and over to the garage. Gertie was waiting there in her sheet, and so was his beacon transmitter—umbrella folded, other components closed in a cardboard box. He looked at it, and wondered momentarily if he really wanted to use it. Might he not be happier in the closet, near Mary, for the rest of his days?

"Okay, E.T., hop on."

They lifted him into the basket of the bike, attached his communicator to the carrying rack over the rear wheel, and pushed off down the driveway, into the street.

He rode in the basket, little legs tucked in, and stared at the parade of Earth children who walked along the street: princesses, cats, clowns, hoboes, pirates, devils, gorillas, vampires, and Frankensteins. Earth was truly an amazing place.

"Hang on, E.T."

Elliott felt the weight of the creature there in the basket—a small but significant being, lost from the stars. Tonight was a mission, and it gave Elliott feelings he'd never had before. As he guided the handlebars and pumped the pedals, bearing E.T.'s weight along, he realized he wasn't a twerp after all. His twerpishness was leaving him, falling behind in the dark and being consumed by the shadows; he knew he was meant for this job, in spite of being nearsighted, sloppy, and depressed. With a surge of his wheels, he felt happy and free, and touched by the hand of outer space. He looked at Michael, and Michael smiled, braces shining on his teeth. He looked at Gertie, and Gertie waved, giggling at how E.T. looked, all crouched up in the basket, furry bedroom slippers sticking out.

We're gonna get him back up where he belongs, thought Elliott, looking toward the Milky Way. It shone through the telephone wires and the pollution, and it seemed to be singing softly. Odd, angling light glanced out of it, sheets and nets of cool flame that reached down and touched him and then danced off and away.

"Why, that's the most incredible costume I've ever seen," said the man in the hallway. His wife was beside him, her eyes open in wonder, their children standing awestruck behind them, peeking out from between their parents' legs at the extraterrestrial.

E.T. had removed his sheet. In his cowboy hat and

bedroom slippers, with his incredible eyes, stomach on the floor, and feet like a toadshade plant, he was certainly in a class by himself as far as Halloweeners went. Each house they'd gone to had been like this, with a big fuss made over him. He liked it. He'd been in a closet for weeks. Now he held out his trick-or-treat basket and received a great deal of candy.

". . . just extraordinary," muttered the man, as he accompanied them back toward the door, eyes glued on E.T.'s long, rootlike fingers, which trailed along the hall carpet.

E.T. stepped onto the sidewalk, with his basket full. What a treasure he'd collected in highest-quality nutritive wafers and drops, enough to carry him for days in space. There were piles of M&Ms, and one especially powerful bar called a Milky Way, apparently for the longer voyages.

"You're a hit, E.T.," said Elliott, wheeling his bicycle along the sidewalk. The space-being waddled along beside him, and Elliott felt the happiness coming from the old creature. Elliott knew what it was to be a freak, laughed at by people; he'd always been that kind of kid, as if his own nose were like a bashed-in Brussels sprout. But he didn't feel that way anymore. He felt older, wiser, and connected to the far-off worlds; great thoughts came and went in his head, like comets, trailing fire and wonder.

As for the aforementioned Brussels sprout, he had begun to notice that certain children were peeking in other people's windows. He tugged at Michael's sleeve and indicated his wishes.

They crept across a lawn, and peeked in a window. A man was walking around in his undershirt, a can of beer in his hand, a cigar in his teeth. The aged space-creature smiled to himself, chin on the windowsill. If he could go out with his friends and peek in windows every night, life on Earth would be worth living.

"Come on, E.T.," whispered Gertie. *"Come on with me . . ."*

She led him quietly around the house, onto the front porch, and across to the door. They pressed the doorbell and ran.

His furry bedroom slippers flapped, one of them fell off, and he lost his cowboy hat. He cried out with joy. He was living now—he was a regular Earth person.

"Faster, faster," called Gertie, and they ducked around some bushes, panting, mist coming out of E.T.'s toes. The old voyager was so excited his fingers worked all by themselves, making cosmic oversigns dealing with the innermost secrets of evolution in the universe. The entire row of bushes swooned, and then bloomed. But the grand old botanist was already gone, to the next house, to soap the windows.

In this way they moved from neighborhood to neighborhood. In the excitement, much candy was devoured and the elderly Halloweener indicated his desire to collect some more.

"Okay," said Elliott. "Let's try that house over there."

Elliott led them up the sidewalk, confident now

that the outrageous figure shuffling beside him would be thought of as just another kid in a rubber costume. As for E.T., he no longer felt strange looking. He'd begun to think of his other-worldly form as just something he'd donned for the evening. Inside he was a human being, eating candy, ringing doorbells, shouting trick-or-treat, and rotating his nose.

But as the door ahead of them opened, his eyes clicked in fear, for the first time all evening, for on the other side of the door was a red-haired little runt he knew at once had to be Lance, about whom he'd always been suspicious.

Lance, for his own part, was very suspicious of E.T. "Who's *this?*" he asked, not assuming that these long arms, this bowling-ball stomach on the doorstep, were made of rubber.

"It's—it's my cousin," stammered Elliott, ready to kick himself for not recognizing Lance's house, where they were now trapped, Lance advancing on them.

"He's plenty weird," said Lance, taking another step closer, drawn by some force he couldn't understand, but deeply in tune with the freakish voyager.

This boy, thought the ancient cosmologist, is a nerd.

He backed up, Elliott backing with him. Lance continued to advance as they retreated, and hopped on his bike as they hopped on theirs.

"Spell *fast,*" said E.T., and Elliott pumped for all he was worth, angry with himself now for being so confident, for showing E.T. off to the world. But how can you keep a secret like E.T. from the world? You want to show him off, want to see people's jaws drop open.

But you shouldn't show him to a nerdy kid like Lance, because nerds can't be fooled. A nerd knows a spaceman when he sees one.

E.T. rode in the bicycle basket, head down, but feet sticking out. What would Lance do? Go to the authorities? Will I, he wondered, be stuffed after all?

Elliott turned and looked over his shoulder, back into the darkness. There was no sign of Lance, who probably couldn't pedal a bike very fast.

"It's okay," he said. "We've lost him."

But they had not lost him. By shortcuts known only to nerds, Lance sped along through the night, ever in touch with his quarry. How did he know just when to turn, and how sharp to cut it? Something was drawing him telepathically. He was tuned, he was in touch with E.T.'s system; he rode like a maniac, faster than the ordinary nerd ever dreams. Red hair pressed flat, jug-ears sticking out, he wheeled like crazy in the moonlight, block after block, on Elliott's trail.

His bicycle light was off, only his reflectors spun patterns in the dark, but no one saw them. Lance felt hot, and cool, and with it, for the first time. In his brief life as a nerdish youth, things never really turned out right, and he'd just shuffled around and played electronic games with himself. But tonight—tonight his bike was boiling with power, he was skidding through turns like a professional rider. His buck teeth clicked with excitement. The wind blew over his cowlick. The night was kind to him.

He bounced over a curbstone, came down squealing his wheels, caught sight of Elliott up ahead, Elliott's tail reflector caught in the glow of a streetlamp near the edge of town.

He's heading for the hills, thought Lance, and smiled to himself as his own bike zoomed beneath the streetlamp, swift and silent, commanded by a cycler who couldn't miss the trail if he tried; he was beaming in, his whole forehead buzzing now.

He leaned over the handlebars, feet spinning the pedals. Deep thoughts of space were appearing in his brain, and he felt he could almost glide into the sky. He smiled again; the kids all laughed at him because he only ate Swiss cheese. But so what? What did that matter now, now that he was floating in this incredible power?

He left the last streetlamp behind and took the high road into the hills.

Elliott looked back over his shoulder but could not see his pursuer. He steered the bike off the highway, onto the fire road, and pedaled up it.

The space-wayfarer bounced in the basket, stomach pressed against the wire, fingers wrapped around it. Now that he was so close to the old landing site, his mind was racing. He must set up his communicator, and begin signaling. Space was vast and time endless; not another moment must be lost. But how slowly Elliott went now, barely moving the bike along.

"Elliott—"

"Yeah?"

"Spell *hang on*." The space-wanderer moved his fingers, releasing a low-level anti-gravity formula, and the bicycle lifted off the ground.

It skimmed the bushes, then the treetops, and sailed on, over the forest.

Better, much better, thought the old voyager, and settled back in his basket.

Elliott was frozen to the handlebars, mouth open, hair standing up. The bike wheels spun slowly in the wind, but his mind spun more quickly as he stared at the forest below. He could see the fire road and the paths through the trees. And above and behind him, the moon, gliding among silver clouds.

Below, an owl was waking up and lazily stretching its wings. It smacked its beak, thinking of mice, or possibly a bat, to munch on. It lifted off into the air and flapped upward nonchalantly. Suddenly its big eyes popped, and it went into a fiercely banking dive.

What in the world—

Elliott and his bike, with a space-goblin in the basket, sailed on by the careening owl, who collapsed his wings and dove to the ground, where he crouched dumbfounded. At that moment, Lance came tearing toward him, and the owl spun around, nearly run down by the advancing nerd.

What's happening to this forest? wondered the bewildered bird, but Lance had no time to answer; he was shooting onward, bike bouncing over roots, stones, branches. His head was filled with electronic beeps, echoing faintly, and he knew where to go, homing in on a secret signal. The forest received him, its pathways opening gently, and the nerd glided through places trained foresters might have gotten jammed in. But where was Elliott?

The moonlight came in webs through the canopy of leaves, above which Elliott sailed, hidden from Lance and the world, sensed only by shocked, squeaking bats on the wing, who darted and dove as the bicycle flew through their domain. Elliott's feet worked the pedals slowly, nervously, the chain clicking in space. He'd always known in his heart that his bike could fly, had sometimes felt it as he crested a hill, but the final touch of magic had always been missing until tonight. E.T. was that magic, and his magic was a science of space so evolved that only the ancient could know it. It assisted their great Ships, and it certainly could carry a mere bicycle a mile or so—to the landing site.

The ancient fugitive peered from his wire basket as the bicycle dropped toward the clearing. He controlled the descent with his delicate touch, and the bicycle slipped in over the grass and touched gently down, spilling only at the last moment when the elderly voyager's long toe got caught in the spokes.

"Ufff . . ."

The bicycle slid on its side, finally stopping on top of E.T. He climbed out of his basket, toe aching, but too excited to care. Elliott was picking himself up, and now began unpacking the communicator.

The ancient voyager turned away for a moment and scanned the clearing, to see if any of those who had pursued him that first night were still lurking about.

His sensitive inner radar moved along, over the face of the forest; it came to Lance and blipped right over him. Why? Because the nerd's emanation was now not unlike E.T.'s own—that of an outcast, a loner, a misfit—and E.T. just swept on by him, feeling no threat.

He turned back to Elliott and signaled that they should begin setting up the transmitter.

The circular saw blade turned like an enchanted dish, beside which knife and fork danced, advancing the teeth of the blade. What caused the enchanted turning? An armature, with spring attached, had been roped into a slender tree. As the wind bent the tree, the rope went taut, lifting the knife-and-fork ratchet; the teeth advanced, spinning the saw blade across which the bobby pins tracked, activating the Speak and Spell program. What powered Speak and Spell? Hundreds of wires, which the ancient botanist had taken into the trees; these wires were now in the veins of leaves, in branches, in roots, tapping the electricity of life; how it was done, only the old botanist knew. But Elliott could feel the life of the forest traveling through the wires, converging, powering the communicator.

The overturned umbrella, lined with tin foil, shone in the moonlight. But more than moonlight was reflected there. The Fuzz Busting microwave signal, driven by the UHF tuner, was beaming out of the parabolic shape, into space.

. . . gleeple doople zwak-zwak snafn olg mnnnnin . . .

... approximately. The true sound coming from the device was far more elegant, but our alphabet cannot convey the subtlety of those sounds E.T. had wrested from the Speak and Spell.

Elliott stood in the flow of the signal, hoping for its success, but it seemed so small, such a feeble thing searching up there in the immensity.

The extraterrestrial, seeing his doubts, touched the boy's shoulder. "We have found a window."

"We have?"

"Our frequency is that window. It will reach Them."

They stood with their transmitter for a long time, both of them silent. The stars seemed to listen too— and of course, the nerd in the bushes was listening.

Mary, meanwhile, was trying to hold her own against the droves of little goblins who were visiting her.

"Yes, yes, come in. My, what a scary bunch this is . . ."

They sang for her, they did little dances. Gooey gumdrops popped out of their mouths in the middle of tunes and were mashed into the rug; tuneful gesturing caused wet lollipops to be pressed into her textured wallpaper, peeling off the texture when they were removed. Harvey bit one of the little goblins. While the fearless watchdog was engaged in this molestation of an innocent child, upstairs a window was being opened in Mary's room, and a government agent was entering with an electronic device, whose flickering light and wavering needle led him down the hall.

The device began to grow excited as it entered Elliott's room, and went quite wild when it was taken into E.T.'s closet. After a few passes, the agent seemed satisfied, and crept back along the hall and out Mary's window, making a safe exit, while downstairs Harvey was having his snout tied with a handkerchief, and the screaming child was being plied with chocolates.

. . . gleeple doople zwak-zwak . . .

Elliott and E.T. sat beside the communicator, listening, and watching the night sky, while Lance the nerd watched them. The sky was silent and did not respond.

After many hours, Elliott fell asleep, and Lance had to be home by nine o'clock, so the old voyager was alone with his device.

He tracked the signal as it spread out and out, into the darkness.

He did not feel so well. Had he eaten too much candy?

He strolled off into the forest, and visited with the plants. His footstep seemed a little heavy to him, heavier than usual. Perhaps it was from all the soaping of windows and running amok. He wasn't used to it.

He walked until he came to a little stream, and he sat down beside it. The sound of the water was enchanting, and he put his head into it. He stayed this way for hours, listening, listening to the artery of

Earth's blood running. He fell asleep finally, head underwater.

"I guess he's about four foot or so," said Mary to the policeman. "A small person, dressed as a hunchback."

She began to weep. "He's eaten a razor blade," she said. "I know it."

"Now, now..." said the policeman. "Lots of kids get lost on Halloween. I'm sure Elliott is fine."

Gray dawn had come to the neighborhood. Gertie and Michael had been home since ten o'clock. Elliott's bed was empty. Mary's mind was in shreds, once again. She stared at the policeman through her tears. "I've been treating him terribly lately. I made him clean his room."

"That's not unreasonable," said the policeman.

Harvey tried to signal, but his snout was still tied shut. He put his paws on the door and made muffled whimpering noises.

"Elliott!" Mary leapt up. Elliott was coming across the back lawn. In gratitude she took off Harvey's muzzle, and the dog yowled with relief, working his jaws up and down.

"Is this our missing person?" smiled the policeman. He folded his notebook, put it away, and left the family to their reunion.

"You've got to find him, Mike. In the forest. Somewhere near the clearing..."

Mary had confined Elliott to bed. And E.T. was the missing person now. Michael went to the garage and took out his bike. In a few minutes he was pedaling down the street, and a car was following him.

Looking back over his shoulder, he saw three figures seated in it, all of them looking intently at him. He cut sharply into a narrow passageway between two houses, shook the car, and headed for the hills.

He found E.T. head-down in the stream. The old voyager did not look good, but he insisted that he was fine, he'd only been listening.

He gestured at the stream, at the sky, and at many things, but to Michael he seemed pale, and his footstep slow and heavy.

"It's only been working a little while," said Michael. "You've got to think positively."

"Tell *him* that," said Elliott, nodding toward the closet, where E.T. sat brooding.

The space-elder knew it was absurd to expect immediate results, or perhaps any results at all. But he couldn't help himself. He'd been dreaming of the Great Ship; as soon as he closed his eyes he saw it, the beautiful ornament descending. But when he woke, he was still alone with nothing but a half-eaten box of Oreos and a stupid, staring Muppet.

Elsewhere in the house, Mary was going about her chores, wondering if life had any answer besides children's sneakers turning up in the refrigerator. Wearily she ran her sweeper, picking up bits of guitar strings and strange-looking seeds that she worried might be from marijuana. Elliott and Michael had been acting very strange lately, and so had Gertie. Was her whole family turning on?

She daydreamed of their father, the irrepressible bum. Gone. To Mexico.

She thought about taking aerobic dancing.

Anyway, buy a new pair of shoes.

But were there any *surprises* left in life for her?

Wasn't everything pretty much the way it was going to be, except wrinkles would be added, and she'd have to buy even more expensive creams to fight them off, made out of placentas or something?

Switching off the vacuum cleaner, she realized the doorbell was ringing.

For some strange reason, her hopes soared. It was crazy, she knew, but the whole house seemed crazy these days. She went toward the door, caught in the idea that her charming bum of a husband would be there, for old time's sake. Or maybe somebody else, for new time's sake. Somebody tall, dark, and devastating.

She opened the door.

It was someone short, red-haired, and nerdish.

"Is Elliott home?"

"Just a minute, Lance..." She sighed, turned, and climbed the stairs toward Elliott's room, which was locked, as usual. What *were* they doing in there? What horrible things to cause her to buy placenta cream before her time...

She knocked. "Elliott, that boy Lance is here."

"He's a nerd. Tell him to get lost."

"I can't do that, Elliott. I'm going to tell him he can come up."

She descended the stairs, feeling they were the treadmill her life had gotten onto. Wouldn't *anything* new come into her situation?

"Thank you," said the nerd, passing her on the stairs. Something incredibly new had come into *his* situation, and he was tracking it, upwards, to the source. His jug-handle ears, which his mother taped down at night, now seemed to swivel still further forward, defeating all of a mother's hopes. He knocked on Elliott's door.

"Let me in."

"Go away . . ."

"I want to see the E.T."

He smiled, greatly satisfied by the effect he could feel his words were having in the suddenly silent room beyond the door.

The door swung open. He stepped, nerd-fashion, intrusively inward. "Listen, let me state my position from the beginning. I admit I was wrong. I do believe in spacemen. I saw one last night, out in the forest, with you."

"I told you," said Elliott, "that was my cousin."

"You have an incredibly ugly family, then. I saw him, Elliott, with my own eyes."

"No, you didn't."

"I don't want to be a tough guy, but there's a man on the block right now, knocking on doors, asking a lot of questions about 'did anybody see anything strange in the neighborhood...'"

"So?"

"So I could walk right up to him now and tell him all I know. And I know a lot." Lance gazed at Elliott, his Swiss-cheese complexion glowing. He was not a bad person, just a born creep. They always seem to show up on days when people are feeling bad, and make them feel worse. "Or I could dummy up. It's your choice."

Elliott sighed, and Lance knew it was surrender. He began to babble. "Where did you find him, Elliott? Do you know where he came from, or what race he is? Is he from our solar system? Does he talk? Has he got any super powers?"

Michael interrupted, "You tell anyone and he'll disintegrate you, you'll just spin around into nothing."

"Can he do that? Really? Has he done it already?"

Elliott walked to the closet, opened it, and stepped in.

The aged monster stared in confusion, for he'd heard Lance's familiar voice, and his mind-probe did not fail him this time. A threatening presence had arrived.

"He's a nerd," said Elliott. "But he won't hurt you. I promise."

E.T. covered his face and shook his head. It was no longer Halloween. His face was not something that could just be shown casually to people.

He was saved by the bell—the doorbell. Elliott and Michael both felt it go off in their nerves, like a wire suddenly growing hot. Elliott backed out of the closet, just in time to see Michael sneaking into the hallway.

The older brother went softly along the hall carpet, then descended silently to the first landing of the stairwell, where he could eyeball the situation below.

The situation had brought Mary from behind the sofa, where she'd found a lifetime supply of spitballs and a magazine that seemed to be devoted to the sex practices of voluptuous space nymphs.

My babies, she thought wearily, my innocent little lost boys.

She walked toward the insistent doorbell, knowing for certain that it would *not* be someone tall, dark, and devastating.

She opened it.

He was tall, dark, and devastating.

But—he was crazy.

". . . investigating rumors of unidentified flying objects . . ."

She stared at the ring of keys hanging from his belt. He certainly had a great many doors to open in life, whoever he was.

Then he showed her what appeared to be a government badge. But couldn't he have gotten it from a cereal box or something?

"I'm sorry," she stammered, "but I don't understand . . ."

"Not far from here, a UFO put down. We have reason to believe one of its crew was stranded . . ."

"You've got to be kidding."

"I assure you—" his eyes penetrated her own "—I'm not."

She gazed back, in wonder. Here she was, divorced, with three kids to support, lonely, frustrated, and thinking of taking dance lessons—when to her door comes an attractive man, possibly single, and looking for flying saucers.

She slumped, just slightly, and fingered her dust-cloth. "Well, I haven't seen anything."

He stared at her, then shifted his gaze beyond her, into the house, as if he already knew a great deal about it, and her, and was just finalizing some elaborate plan. If he tried to push past her, she'd brain him with the dust mop, then nurse him back to health.

But now he was apologizing for bothering her, and backing down the steps. She watched him go along the sidewalk, and wondered if he'd read too many comic books as a child. Or had he taken a bad fall?

Then she noticed a sleek, government-style car pulling in to the curbstone alongside him. The driver gave him a sort of salute, and the man climbed in, joining some other men in the back seat.

Had they all taken a bad fall?

She stepped away from the hall window, and resumed her intimate relationship with the dust mop. Maybe she had misjudged the caller. Maybe he was a serious person, with a serious mission.

Yeah, sure, and there's a spaceman in the closet.

She opened it, arranged the scattered overshoes, coats, hats, gloves. The umbrella was still missing. She knew Michael and Elliott had taken it; she just hoped it wasn't being used for anything pornographic.

Michael snuck back into Elliott's room. "He's an investigator. He showed Mom a badge. He says there have been UFOs..."

Lance bounced up and down, as if upon springs. "Did you see a UFO? You must be the luckiest person in the world."

Elliott interrupted. "Did she tell him anything?"

"No."

"Does he know about the communicator?"

Lance bounced some more. *"That's* what it is! Did he bring it from some other world? Is it like a real future machine?"

"He made it out of bobby pins."

"Bobby pins?" Lance fumbled with this momentarily, then pressed on, as a nerd will. "Is he trying to reach his planet? Oh, God, Elliott, are they going to land? Where? When?" Then, feeling that he was losing position, he renewed his threat. "Show me the E.T. right now, or I'll run after the guy with the badge. I mean it."

"Do you know that you suck?"

"I can't help myself."

Elliott, knowing he had to do it, opened the door.

The monster stepped forth, calm once more, lost in his own thoughts and munching an Oreo. He looked at the nerd.

Lance's hands dropped limply to his sides. The blood ran completely out of his cheeks, leaving them the color of white American cheese still wrapped in plastic. A variety of beeping noises sounded behind his brow, the same sounds he'd heard on his moonlight ride. "I could die today," he said in a whisper, "and go to heaven."

"You might," said Michael. "You're going to make a blood oath."

"Anything," said Lance, hardly knowing or caring about Michael, Elliott, or the world. Because here before him was the most incredible being on earth. "I've...dreamt...about you..." said Lance, softly, "...all my life..."

Michael grabbed Lance by the wrist. "Say after me: I swear I will never tell a living soul what I have seen today."

Michael's pocket knife cut into his own finger, and into Lance's, as Lance muttered, "I swear..."

Blood flowed from their fingers, and Michael pressed them together. The cosmic voyager, watching in puzzlement, raised his own finger, which began glowing pink.

"No," said Elliott, "don't."

It was too late. The pinkish glow spread outward, touching Michael and Lance. The cuts in their fingers stopped bleeding, the skin fused back together, and the wounds were healed without a trace.

Everyone on his staff called him Keys. He had a name, but his keys were his real signature: keys to an ordinary looking warehouse with a lot of extraordinary rooms inside, to which he also held the keys.

He stood in one of these rooms now, in front of an operations map on which concentric circles were drawn, ever narrowing, to a single point.

He addressed his assistant, quietly, his eyes remaining on the map. "I heard some religious fanatics on the radio the other day. Talking about our sighting. They claim the Ship is a Satanic manifestation."

The assistant drank black coffee, and continued working on the roster slip before him. It was a list of names, most of which had scientific credentials after them: doctors, biologists, laboratory specialists of every kind. "You know, don't you, that once we bring these people into the act, your chances of looking like an idiot grow at an astonishing rate?"

"It's *time* to bring them in," said Keys, eyes still on the map, on the point that was Elliott's house.

His assistant looked up from the roster. "But suppose the children are just imagining it all? Suppose what we picked up on the snooper is just a kid's game?"

"The Ship landed here." Keys pointed at one of the outer circles. His finger came back along the inner circles. "We picked up conversation about a stranded crewmember here." He put his finger on the dot that was Elliott's house. "It's too close to be a coincidence."

Keys reached behind him and pressed the button of a tape recorder, and Elliott's voice sounded on the tape:

"*. . . from far away in space, Michael, from a place we can't begin to understand. We've got to help him . . .*"

Keys pressed the *stop* button and the operations room was quiet again. He'd felt the awesomeness of the Ship the night it landed, had seen its incredible approach on his tracking screen: an amazing power-package from the stars, sinking over the horizon. The Ship's performance conformed to the pattern his agency was familiar with from other sightings. Only this time the Ship had been taken by surprise.

His assistant rose from the desk and joined him at the map. "All right," he said, tapping the roster slip with his finger, "this is everyone you want. It reads like a Nobel Prize banquet."

"Round them up."

"Will you listen to me for just one second? Before we involve the scientific community?" The assistant turned to the map. "*If* a crewmember was left behind, it doesn't seem likely he'd be hiding in somebody's *house*."

"Why not?"

"Because he's an *alien being*. He'd be handling himself guerrilla-style, out in the hills." The assistant pointed to the terrain he thought likely to be sheltering whatever it was they'd been chasing. "You think they have no training in survival? You think the intelligence behind that ship never planned on such a contingency?"

"We caught them with their pants down," said Keys, quietly.

"Maybe we did. But if you were an alien being, would *you* go knocking on doors in the nearby neighborhood?"

"He's in that house," said Keys.

"Let's find that out for sure before we ring in this crowd." The assistant tapped the roster again. "It's going to be a three-ring circus once these people arrive. There'll be no way to plug leaks. And if you've guessed wrong, if that house has nothing in it but a couple of goofy kids with a Space Invaders mentality, *you* are going to be out of a job. Because you will have spent about ten million bucks on a wild-goose chase. The government is cutting the budget, remember? We operate on the fringes."

Keys pointed at the roster. "Round them up."

The assistant sighed. "If you're wrong, we can both look forward to careers gathering evidence for divorce courts. The motel unit of some sleazy private eye outfit..." He started to turn away, then turned back, pointing at the outermost circles of the map, the forests and hills. "Your man, if he's anywhere, is up in these hills, eking out a marginal existence."

"Robinson Crusoe, I suppose."

"That's right. Certainly not sitting in somebody's kitchen having a milkshake."

E.T. sat in the kitchen, sipping his milkshake through a straw. The straw, he felt, was one of the finest inventions on Earth, making drinking so much easier.

"You like that, E.T.?" asked Elliott, across from him at the table.

The alien being nodded, as the delicious liquid gurgled in his glass.

The roster was called up: a scattered group of specialists who had previously been investigated, given security clearance, and then asked to sign themselves on to a most peculiar standby group; this they did, some with amusement, some with scorn, all of them idly, never dreaming their expertise would someday actually be required. So it was with great surprise that each of them listened to a voice somewhere on the other end of the telephone line, and it was with a profound quiet that they finally laid the phone back into its cradle, staring at it and wondering who was crazy, they or the government.

In its hidden spot near the landing site, the communicator continued to send its constant signal, out, out, out, into space. It had no patent, it wasn't licensed, and it looked like something you might find at a public dump. But as Elliott approached, he felt the energy that powered it, and knew this pile of spare parts had class.

Night had fallen, and he was alone with the thing. Its ratchet-wheel clicked faintly in the grass, like a kind of cricket, calling to another.

Elliott lay back in the grass and stared up at the star-filled sky. He lay for a long time, just a little punk kid with a head mostly filled with trash, but he had come to like starlight. At times the moon seemed to open out with a great yellow light and then a shimmering veil would flow between the stars. A soft voice would speak an unintelligible word—or was it just the wind?

He listened to the transmitter, to the code that was beyond him but went all through him anyway; the overturned umbrella shining with moonlight, shone into him.

Inside his head, he could hear Mary wondering where he was, what he was doing out so late, but he just switched her off and spread his arms in the grass. The stars worked their veils of light, subtle streams of loveliness, moving, hypnotizing him. He lay for hours, caught by forces he couldn't resist, forces he was never supposed to have known, that no one on Earth was to have shared.

Elliott shivered, not from cold, but from the feelings that were starting to move through him. Cosmic loneliness had gotten into the marrow of his Earthbones.

He moaned in the grass, under a heavy burden, for Earthlings weren't ready for the hunger of the stars.

The voice whispered this to him, opening his youthful mind, wider, wider.

Still bound to their planet, Earthlings can't deal with the ache of universal love, said the golden whisper echoing through the endless corridors.

Elliott stared at the night sky and seemed to go out of himself, into the starshine of old, so sweetly alluring yet whose secrets are hidden from men, and wisely so. He rolled on the grass, body buzzing with cool starfire. The message shot through his whole being—a message meant to be carried by a creature much more evolved than himself, a creature whose inner nature was such that it could love a star and be loved in return by the overwhelming solar force.

The music of the spheres devoured him, taking his meager little Earth-soul and overwhelming it with the ecstasy of the cosmos, against which Earthlings by birth are shielded.

He choked back a sob, climbed to his feet, staggered over to his bike. He couldn't take it, couldn't deal with the images that were starting to cascade over him, of space-time, of the unbearable, unthinkable curve.

He pedaled, reflectors turning, little moons at his feet, round and round, round and round. He bounced down the fire road, shaking in every limb.

Keys' office had photos on all the walls; the caption beneath each photo identified the print as belonging to the Air Force. While some of the shots were merely blurs of light—beautiful streaks moving horizontally or vertically across the sky—others were clear enough to make a man believe, especially when the photographers happened to be Air Force reconnaissance pilots with a low margin for hallucination and none for darkroom hocus-pocus.

Upon Keys' desk was a plaster cast of E.T.'s footprint, taken from the soft ground of the landing site. Beside it was a portfolio containing an analysis of the traces of fuel emission left at the site by the Ship.

Keys, therefore, was not some drunk in the moonlight, nor a frustrated zany, nor a professional hoaxer. He was a reasonably well-paid government employee who, at the moment, was on the telephone with a figure far above himself in the hierarchy, to whom he was giving his assurances that the agency he headed was about to earn its salary.

"It will take several more days...no, the delay is unavoidable...we're following the original directive, that the specimen be given a complete life-support system..."

Keys listened, nodded, drummed his fingers, gave another assurance. "The area is under surveillance and no one, nothing, can get by us now...yes, very good..."

He hung up the phone. It was night, during the last calm before the storm. He sipped his coffee. If he was wrong, if the net closed on nothing but air, he would most definitely be out of a job. But it would be a glorious couple of hours.

The door opened and his assistant entered. "The Quarantine and Contamination Unit is enormous. The entire house will have to be screened."

"So?"

"So have you ever seen a plastic tent the size of a house? With tubes sticking out of it? We're going to be the weirdest-looking sight in five counties, and

about a million people are going to show up, I promise."

"They won't get through."

Keys' assistant looked down into the plaster print
of E.T.'s foot. "Why don't we just glide in, grab the
spaceman, and vanish? A low-profile operation."

"I might prefer it that way," said Keys, "but that's
not the way *they* want it." He pointed to the telephone.

"Sure, because they want to ride the publicity if
the spaceman is there. But if he's not—if we storm
this neighborhood with the kind of equipment you've
got here—" he tapped another sheaf of papers "—we
are going to traumatize a lot of people. Who will sue
the government. Bear it in mind." The assistant turned
and left.

Keys bore it in mind. But it was only in a corner
of his mind. Because he knew the spaceman was there.
He lit a cigarette, blew smoke toward the ceiling, and
tossed the dead match into E.T.'s plaster footprint.

Government vehicles rolled; a certain warehouse
opened its doors, and uniformed attendants waved
equipment into the voluminous depths of the building.

Keys checked it all, and checked in those whose
job it was to reassemble and run the equipment. The
interior of the warehouse started to resemble a military
hospital.

• • •

E.T. opened the closet door and Elliott fell in, onto the pillows. His eyes were swollen, his lips trembling with star-words he couldn't pronounce. He sat, sobbing to himself, as the aged guest looked on.

The space creature touched Elliott's forehead. The gathered influence of the galaxies withdrew, whirling away, out to the denizens of deep space for whom it was intended. Elliott slouched down, sighing from the toes. In a few minutes he was asleep, in a cocoon through which the star-bane could not shine.

The old voyager looked at the sleeping child, and felt a bittersweet feeling in his own body, an ache and a joy that he could not understand; but then he understood, that he loved this child.

I am his guide and protector, though what have I guided him to? To the dark lunacy of the night. And what have I taught him?

To steal from the hardware store.

But Elliott—he touched the boy's forehead again— my heart-light is brighter because of you. You are *my* teacher, my guide and protector. Has there ever been such a child as this?

So selfless and serving?

May every star bless you with gentle knowing, of the sort you can receive, use, and understand.

He made hand signs of command to the subtle flow of moon and starlight, and bent it gently around Elliott's sleeping form.

A sniffing at the crack of the door indicated that Harvey the dog had arrived, for his nightly sojourn with E.T.

The space-goblin opened the door and Harvey slunk in sideways, still not perfectly secure. He sniffed the sleeping Elliott, then circled a pillow several times, and finally sat down in front of E.T.

E.T. gazed at him and the dog gazed back shiftily, but their gazes continued to merge. Gradually, Harvey's tongue fell out, and one ear curled, as he saw, in his doggie-mind, the Great Cosmic Bone, floating in the soup of space. His tongue flicked over his chops and he made a low whining noise.

E.T. instructed him further, in telebeams of light, mind to mind, about things a dog should know while howling at the moon.

Mary stood in front of the filing cabinet, thumbing through the folders. It was only eleven and her feet were already killing her. She looked at the pile of papers yet to be filed. She would have liked to file them in the airshaft, a lovely fluttering storm of correspondence.

"Mary, when you get a chance, would you run these ideas down to the sales department?"

When I get a chance? She looked at her employer. He was a dumbbell, a tyrant, a sadist, and a fool. If he were single, she'd marry him. So she could sit down.

"Yes, Mr. Crowder, I'll get to it just as soon as I can."

"And while you're at it, could you—"

"Yes, I'd be glad to."

"But I didn't tell you what it was yet." A puzzled frown came to Crowder's forehead.

"I'm sorry, Mr. Crowder, I thought the filing cabinet was about to tip over. It does that occasionally."

"It does?"

"If you open all the drawers at once."

Crowder was temporarily sidetracked by this, and stood gazing at the cabinet. She frequently wondered how, without qualifications of any kind, he'd risen to the position he held in the corporation, but more frequently she wondered how she held the position she did, without going insane. She was thinking of quitting. Maybe she'd quit today and go to work in a gas station. Mechanics always seemed to have a sense of humor, especially when they were working on her car.

"You say, if you open all the drawers?" Crowder was examining the cabinet.

"I wouldn't advise you to try."

"But we should—fasten it to the wall, shouldn't we?"

"Possibly." More interesting, thought Mary, would be Mr. Crowder fastened to the wall. And used as a bulletin board.

"I must tell maintenance about this." Crowder marched off, sidetracked until lunchtime. Mary spent it on a bench in the park, eating a submarine sandwich and massaging her instep. Beside her on the bench, an elderly woman was having a conversation with someone inside her shopping bag.

Mary looked at her; she'd probably been a file clerk.

And this is how I'm going to end up. Having a meaningful relationship with a paper bag.

She stretched her legs out and sighed. If only Mr. Right would come along with his own Visa card. She closed her eyes and tried to imagine him.

But she kept getting the image of someone no bigger than an umbrella stand, waddling toward her with a candy bar.

"Traveling on business, are you?" asked the fellow passenger at thirty thousand feet.

"Ah, yes," said the microbiologist. "A convention..."

Elliott opened his locker in the basement of the school, and tossed his books in, papers spilling out, notes falling any old way. He stared dejectedly at the jumble, wanting to make some kind of effort toward learning, but schoolwork wasn't starshine, it was sludge. He swung the locker door closed and walked down the hallway. The gray walls of the school were as cheerful as jail. And Lance, Nerd of the Year, was coming toward him.

He'd brought along a *Time* magazine mirror. He framed Elliott's face in it. "The Boy of the Year, friend of presidents and kings and—E.T.s." He slid it over so that the mirror now included his own face. "Of course, somebody else will be on there with you. We know who, don't we, sort of pink, with blue eyes?"

This tasteless speech, so typical of a nerdling, had the expected effect, of making the flesh crawl. Elliott's was crawling, with a desire to kick Lance in the pants.

Lance smiled, feeling that he was finally getting somewhere in the world. With his face on the cover of *Time,* he could go straight from the fifth grade into the aerospace program and give advice on communicating with extraterrestrials, for wasn't his head beeping constantly with just such messages?

"He's talking to me, Elliott, all the time. He *likes* me."

"I wonder why."

"He senses that I can be useful. Elliott—" Lance took Elliott by the sleeve. "Do you realize that we're the most important people in this school, at this moment? Because we're *in touch.*" Lance's squinty eyes became more so, like a nocturnal squirrel of the flying variety, out in daylight.

Elliott looked into those beady, watery eyes and had to admit—the glow of E.T. was there. He couldn't kick Lance in the pants, much as he'd love to.

"Yeah, right, Lance, it's true. We're in touch. Hey, I've gotta go . . ."

He moved off down the hall, and Lance went his own way, both of them buzzing, but Elliott buzzing more so, and the buzz was not a happy one; the cosmic loneliness had returned in a wave that was coming through the wall of the school. Tracing it to the source was not a difficult matter: from the wall of the school, go across town, turn right, go up toward the hills, to the little collection of houses there, and enter one of them; in the upstairs closet an elderly space voyager is sitting with his geranium, deep in despair.

"...extraterrestrial," muttered the microbiologist, as he was escorted down the hallway toward the briefing room. He turned to a colleague, in step beside him. "I'm sorry now I signed onto this damned roster."

"Oh, well," said the fellow scientist, "I needed a vacation."

"The government," said the microbiologist, "can think of more ways to waste a man's time..."

They entered the briefing room, where the table was already filled, smoke curling overhead, scientific, military, and medical personnel seated together, their voices a low rumble.

A soft jingle of keys announced the entry of the team leader, who walked to the head of the table. Silence came almost at once.

"Ladies and gentlemen, we won't keep you long. I know you're tired from travel and you must rise before dawn tomorrow. The system of quarantine we're employing is elaborate and will take considerable preparation..."

• • •

What sort of fellow was Keys, this quiet man at the center of a cyclone that was gradually picking up speed?

He'd had this odd dream as a child: that a spacecraft would come to Earth and select him as the recipient of its advanced knowledge. He would then turn this knowledge over to humanity.

The dreams of childhood seldom come true. Keys' dream kept moving him into ever more recondite arenas of surveillance, until finally he was one of those who looked for that which was most obscure of all—a flashing light in the sky, a trail of vapor on the horizon, a troubling shape on a radar screen.

Keys became a man familiar with deserts and mountaintops, had spent months on them, with the full map of stars overhead, through which the mystery sailed, maddeningly distant.

But like every hunter who is diligent, Keys gradually saw a pattern in the movement of his prey. He was outclassed in every way; he rode in a jeep while his quarry commanded a comet of power; he had to be satisfied with Earth technology, when the craft above him moved with inhuman grace. But habit seems universal, and Keys discovered that even the celestial captain had one—which had to do with the cycle of Earth's vegetation.

Gradually, Keys came to this peculiar realization: the great Ship arrived when things blossomed.

So Keys followed the blossoms—and now, on his office wall, was a photograph of the Ship, taken closeup as it had blasted off in the hills behind Elliott's house.

Outside his office, the warehouse now buzzed with activity as more specialists arrived, and technicians, and their backup teams. It was a trap that closed slowly, too slowly for Keys, but every piece had to be in place, so that the trophy wouldn't be spoiled.

Within the warehouse was every available life-support system—for a dead spaceman was not the prize. The prize was a living trophy, and Keys had done all in his power to ensure that this one would be kept alive. Whatever shock it had sustained from prolonged time in an alien environment, Keys had the antidote. All that medical science had created, Keys had in his warehouse. Whatever Earth had to offer, it would offer the stranded member of the alien crew.

Keys had not considered that too much expertise might be dangerous, that a little spaceman who thrived on M&Ms did not need intravenous feeding, nor a possible organ transplant.

But Keys closed the only net of which he had ever conceived—a gigantic one, every knot in it an expert of some kind, and the entire thing able to restore life to a dead and frozen mastodon if it had to, to awaken any organ, rejuvenate any cell, sustain anything, from any conceivable atmosphere in the universe.

"I don't want a dead spaceman," was the order that went out continually to his colleagues, and to the gathering crew.

But already there was a smothering amount of

equipment being assembled; if every one of the test-wires that now dangled at the ready were attached to E.T.'s body, he would look like a telephone switchboard. And everyone in the warehouse wanted desperately to attach themselves to the creature they'd heard about. Who wouldn't?

Keys' gigantic net was electric—incandescent—ready to be wrapped around a three-foot-tall creature hiding in a closet. And somehow, the creature knew.

The geranium was drooping, as was E.T., head down, hands folded like a pair of dead squid in his lap. All hope for his communicator had left him. It had been running for weeks, and there was no answer from space. The crew of the Great Ship was far off, speeding fast, gone beyond recalling.

I'm dying, Master, whispered the geranium faintly, but the old botanist could do nothing; the plant was absorbing his emotions, and over those he had no control. Cosmic loneliness had gotten to the marrow of his bones.

He leaned on the Muppet, pushed himself up off the creature's head, and looked out the closet window. His gaze went off into the sky, telescopically focusing through the blue, but there was no glint of Ship, no halo of energy, no trail of vapor. A plane went by, trailing the advertisement of a nearby shopping mall, where a pair of orangutans would be on exhibit for shoppers that afternoon.

He turned away. In a short time, he too would be

on exhibit. Stuffed, shellacked, and set on a shelf. Perhaps a few varnished Oreo cookies would be placed beside him to show on what the creature fed.

He opened the closet door and stepped out into Elliott's room. Wearily he took a path through the boy's piled-up clutter. Deeply depressed, he stepped into the hallway.

Broken in spirit, he descended the stairs, duck feet flapping on the carpet runners.

He stood in the downstairs hallway, feeling the inner pulse of the house. It was a chaotic, crazy place, but he loved it. How he wished he could bring riches to it, and the answer to everyone's dreams, but all he was capable of was making the furniture float in the air, and what was the good of that? It would only make it difficult to get into a chair.

He shuffled down the hallway, his form no taller than the umbrella stand. It was giving him a complex, but with all his other problems, what did it really matter?

He entered the kitchen and opened the refrigerator.

What could an extraterrestrial eat today?

He had a strange urge to eat Swiss cheese.

Moo, said the cheese.

"Moo," said the ancient guest, and made himself a sandwich, with mustard.

What will I drink with this creation, he wondered, and finally chose a bright bottle.

He sat at the kitchen table, dined, and drank.

His tongue ran a quick analysis of the components of the beverage: malted barley, hops, adjuncts of rice and corn. Should be perfectly harmless.

He drank it down, found it much to his liking, and drank another.

The sun splashed its light across the kitchen table. He gazed at the window. It appeared to rotate slightly, first left, then right.

What a peculiar sensation.

He opened another bottle of the beverage and poured it down his throat, nonstop, enjoying the little gurgling sound it made.

Then he stood and found he could not walk.

It's happened, he said to himself as he clutched the edge of the table. The gravity of Earth is finally weighing me down.

His knees buckled, just as he'd feared they would when the time came, when the pressure grew too great for his frame. His feet were going in opposite directions, his ankles felt like mush. He bumped into the stove, bounced back, crashed into the doorway.

His hands flailed about limply in the air, wrist joints apparently in deterioration too.

He staggered into the living room, stomach dragging over the rug in a somewhat lower profile than was usual. He wished he had wheels on his stomach; he imagined them, one on each side, with reflectors on them.

He switched on the TV set.

"... *reach out,*" sang the TV. "... *reach out and touch someone.*"

He stared stupidly at the screen, eyelids blinking slowly.

The telephone rang. He reached out his squidlike

hand, gripped the phone as he'd seen Elliott do, and picked it up. From within the instrument came the voice of a woman whose voice-pattern was like Mary's, but older, naggier, and somewhat nutty.

"Hello, Mary? I only have a minute, but I wanted to give you this recipe I know you'll love, and it has things in it you should be getting more of, what with your unbalanced diet..."

"...reach out," sang the TV, *"...reach out and just say hi."*

"Say hi," said the drunken old goblin.

"Elliott? Is this my little angel-eyes? What are you doing home from school? Are you sick? This is your grandma, honey."

"Spell mechanic."

"You should be in bed, Elliott. You get right back into bed this minute. Ask your mother to call me later."

"Call me later."

"You get better, sweetheart. Stay warm." The scatterbrained old zany made kissing sounds into the receiver.

The potted old botanist returned them and lowered the phone back to its base.

He opened another bottle of beer, put his feet up, and continued watching the TV screen.

Humming drunkenly to himself, he tapped his feet back and forth against each other. Forgotten was the fact that his telepathic sender was on full force, and that flowing from his very pickled brain was a very plastered wave.

It swerved around the room, bumped through the

wall, and sailed off across town, looping and swaying, until it reached the school, where it paused once, and then charged.

Elliott was leaning in over the biology work table when the tipsy, wobbling wave hit.

The teacher was speaking. "Now in front of each position is a glass jar. I am going to come around and put a piece of cotton, soaked in ether, in each jar, and then we will deposit our frog into the same jar and wait for it to expire."

Elliott swayed, sank forward, and put his lips to the bottle. He began making space-noises, indefinable but most definitely befuddled, like the ones the soused old space-warp was himself making at that very moment—burbles, babbles, and bleats.

"The comedian," said the teacher, "will please silence himself."

This Elliott attempted to do, but the room seemed bent out of shape, and so was he. Trying to compose himself, he looked at the girl next to him at the table, a certain Peggy Jean, who seemed to have enjoyed his noises of the previous moment. She gave him a faint smile, and he returned it, lips feeling as if made out of Silly Putty.

"Very well..." The teacher prepared the cotton, soaking it with ether.

Elliott returned his gaze to the frog bottle. The frog was looking out at him, and for the first time, Elliott saw that E.T. himself looked very much like a frog, a short, squat space traveler in a jar, staring helplessly out.

"You're not gonna kill that poor defenseless thing, are you?" said Elliott.

"I am," said the teacher.

Meanwhile, back at the TV set, the short, squat space traveler was watching an afternoon soap opera. Harvey the dog had come in through his doggie-door and was sitting beside E.T., hoping in dumb-doggie fashion that the monster would give him further instructions in the ways of space-time, and some of his sandwich.

On the TV screen, the soap-hero had just bent the soap-heroine over, and was presenting her with a passionate kiss.

E.T. looked at Harvey.

Harvey gave a low, cowering whine.

The besotted old monster reached out, embraced the muddled mongrel, and placed a kiss upon his snout.

Elliott turned to Peggy Jean, bent her backward over the desk, and placed a passionate kiss upon her lips.

The teacher went berserk, with some justification, for now Elliott was running from bottle to bottle, releasing the popeyed prisoners, who did not hesitate to vacate the premises at once, hopping along the floor and out the door.

"Heal!" cried Elliott, quite out of his mind by now, and speaking biblically. Perhaps he was tuning in to other waves, from special-interest TV channels. In any case, he was running through the classroom, shouting, "Out, you poison demons, in the name of

God!" Which advice the last lingering frogs took, by catapulting leaps to the windowsill.

Tyler stretched his long legs under the worktable and shook his head sadly. For the first time since he'd known Elliott, he sort of felt sorry for him; Elliott had changed, wasn't a stingy little rat like he used to be. In fact, he was almost a good guy. Except he was flipping out. "Sir, sir," said Tyler, trying to divert the teacher from Elliott, "a frog just hopped in your lunch bag."

The teacher swerved from his course, grabbed the bag, and shook it, spilling out his sandwich, the contents falling into a formaldehyde solution, ham and cheese sinking down, instantly pickled. No frog was visible. The last one was being assisted off the windowsill at the back of the room, by Greg, who was foaming at the mouth with excitement. The frog sailed through the air, followed by a perfect floating spit-bubble, radiant in the sunlight.

Elliott was dragged from the room by the enraged teacher. Steve took out his winged hat, put it on, and wiggled the wings. "Suspension for sure," he said, and gave more deep thought to the things that could happen to you when your kid sister got in control of your life.

The real control behind Elliott's fit of madness was just now drunkenly switching channels on the TV set. E.T., plastered out of his mind, settled back into the living room chair, his short legs sticking straight off the end of the cushion. The news came on, spoiling the afternoon with an account of a mine cave-in.

"*. . . the south tunnel collapsed,*" a dust-covered rescuer was saying into a microphone. "*I think we have everyone out, but these men are in critical condition.*"

A closeup of the injured miners was flashed to the afternoon world. In his easy chair, the tipsy little goblin lifted his finger. It began glowing pink.

The injured men leapt off their stretchers. They threw their arms around each other, crying with amazement as they held up their healed arms and legs.

The spaceman opened another bottle of beer.

Elliott's teacher dragged him down the hall, fed up with his behavior. A biology teacher's life is no bed of roses; the hordes of pimply adolescents he dealt with each day had pretty much shattered his nerves; on occasion, he'd thought of putting his own head in the ether. Certainly he would have liked to put Elliott's in the solution. Fighting down this homicidal urge, he settled for turning Elliott over to the principal, with hopes that the principal would flog him, or have him flogged. Of course, such things are not done in a modern school system, and the trembling, broken biology teacher reeled out of the principal's office, feeling that ultimately the children would win, sacrificing him on his own lab table, with cotton wads up his nose and a red incision down his torso.

Within the principal's office, moderation, as indicated above, was being practiced. The principal, a forward-thinking educator, took out his briar pipe, lit it, and attempted to produce an atmosphere of mutual confidence. "Tell me what it is, son. Pot? Quaaludes? Angel wings?"

He extinguished his match and puffed gently. "Your generation, my boy, is going to hell in a hand-basket. You have to take responsibility for your life..."

The principal was off and running; he enjoyed the sound of his own voice as much as the next person, and the fact of a completely captive audience, Elliott, who dared not move, was reassuring to him. He flogged the boy with clichés, strings of them, taken from television, newspapers, boring professional journals, and the sparkling shallows of his own mind. "...understand that in this day and age, one must pull oneself up by one's own bootstraps..."

His pipe sent out contented little puffs. The world was firmly in place. Rebellious youth would soon see that it did no good to rock the boat. "...you can't fight the system, son, it doesn't get you anywhere. It *doesn't make sense*..." He pointed with his pipe-stem for emphasis. His predecessor in the office had been a sexual offender, retired early after several private incidents in the supply closet became public. *He'd* rocked the boat. The office of principal now, however, was stable; a predictable atmosphere prevailed. The pillars of education were unshakable; the earth had been tamed. The system would prevail.

Except that Elliott had started to float out of his chair.

It was E.T.'s fault, of course. His drunken wavelength was still acting up, bouncing around the principal's office, and finally, as seen now, buoying poor Elliott upward like a loose cork.

Elliott gripped the arms of his chair with all his might and forced himself back down; the principal didn't notice, thought the boy was merely squirming.

". . . this fairy-tale approach to life you and your friends have *is costing you valuable time*. Do you see what I'm driving at?" He went on jawing, oblivious of Elliott, captivated by his own drone. ". . . the world is a *known quantity*, son. Stop looking in the cobwebs. Stop daydreaming about things that don't exist. This, I think, is the *root* of all your problems."

The root of Elliott's problems was that he was being uprooted from the gravitation of Earth. The tipsy wave was under his bottom again, playfully bearing him upward with a force that now broke Elliott's grip on the chair. Without further notice, he floated up to the ceiling of the principal's office.

The principal was cleaning his glasses, gaze averted as he held the lenses to the light and droned on. ". . . predictable behavior, my boy. Do you know what tremendous advances have been made because mankind found that matter behaved in predictable ways?"

He looked toward Elliott's chair.

Elliott was not there.

He was floating at the ceiling, a fact discerned a moment later by the principal, whose eyeballs grew considerably more convex at the discovery. He pressed back deeply into his swivel chair, tightened fingers popping a lens out of his glasses. A lifetime of clichés seemed to be raining over him in a shower of tinkling noises, as if a skylight had collapsed on his head. His nose was swelling—perhaps it was going to bleed—and his mind felt like a sock suddenly turned inside out. He signaled for silence, but no one was speaking. It was just a boy, floating on the ceiling that made his ears ring as if anvils were going off in them, as if multitudes were shouting, as if a train had just passed over him, wheels clickety-clacking.

He collapsed deeper into his chair and, like Harvey the dog, a whining noise escaped his lips.

Elliott slowly descended into his chair once more.

"May I go now, sir?"

"Yes, yes, please go . . ." The principal waved him away, and swiveled slowly toward the window where the sunlight danced. Then he swiveled back, opened his *Confiscated Drugs* drawer and swallowed a handful of Quaaludes.

Back at its source, the drunken wave was strongest, as the soused old space-being flapped about the house. He'd finished the sixpack of beer; to a resident of Earth, it was not a great deal of alcohol to have running around in one's system. To this sawed-off, finely tuned, ages-old, innocent creature of the sky, it was like a ton of bricks.

Bumping into things, overturning others, he bumbled around from room to room, Harvey the dog following faithfully.

Harvey himself was in bad shape, owing to his own telepathy; his normally bouncing dogtrot was now a half-loaded stagger, and the poor beast slid under a chair, crawled out with effort, and then fell splay-legged under the sofa.

"What's wrong with you?" asked the old monster. "Can't you walk straight? Walk like me..." E.T. demonstrated, rolling over the hassock.

Dogs generally enjoy foolish behavior, but Harvey was seeing little soup bones floating all around him, along with spaceships labeled *Ken-L Ration* blinking on and off; he bit at them, only to find, to his frustration that they were not there.

E.T. rolled back and forth on the hassock awhile, then pushed off and tried a few disco steps Gertie had taught him, as he sang, "Accidents will happennnnn..."

He sang on key but he did something to the tone values, so that radiant over-echoes filled the air. Harvey whimpered, hearing great long caverns of stone, hewn in far-off worlds where little monsters came and went.

"...but it's only rocks and rolling..."

The monster swayed, attempting to Hustle his bowling ball of a stomach. This bizarre display of dancing prowess might have gone on longer, except for Mary returning home. She came through the front door, leafed through a magazine at the mail table, then stepped toward the kitchen.

The aged space-hero decided the time had come for presenting his love to her. He could hear her, feel her every thoughtwave; she was ready for a mature creature like himself.

He stepped into the hallway.

Harvey, though being bombarded by strange dreams himself, knew this was madness.

He leapt after E.T., just as Mary turned their way. The dog went up on his hind legs in front of the monster, and sat begging, tongue out, straining every part of his dog's-body to block the space monster from Mary's view.

As stated previously, E.T. was not an overlarge being, about the height of an umbrella stand, and Harvey was able to cover this much with his own pawing, begging, tongue-out form.

"Why, Harvey," said Mary, "I didn't know you could beg so well. Did Elliott teach you that?"

The dog nodded.

"But I don't feed you till later, Harvey, you know that." Mary walked off, back down the hall and out the door to her garden.

Harvey collapsed from his excruciating beg-posture; never one to overexert mind or body, he had not fully enjoyed his performance. He looked at the old space monster.

The old monster looked at him, and looked past him, toward the door to the garden. E.T. had decided it was senseless to hide his wisdom from Mary, and that now was the hour to win her with song, story, and cosmic finger signals of the more intimate kind.

He pushed Harvey aside.

The dog up-gravitied and came down two steps to the right, just as Mary came back in with an armful of flowers.

Harvey leaped in front of E.T., and whipped his tail with much force. E.T. had one foot off the floor, eager to go forward; off balance in this way, and half crocked or more, he was knocked across the hall by the swiping tail, and through an open doorway.

Harvey again assumed the beg-posture, knees killing him, but holding it anyway, as Mary stopped, covered in blossoms and seeing nothing.

"Harvey, you're certainly active today." She turned and looked at him. "Did Michael put speed in your Alpo?"

The dog nodded.

Mary continued on by, and set the flowers on the kitchen table, where she picked up an armload of dry-cleaning, swiveled it over her shoulder and headed for the stairs. *Did I see that dog nod?*

E.T. struggled to his feet, bracing himself against a chair. He seemed to be bouncing all around the house, getting nowhere. It was worse than navigating an asteroid belt. He swayed, took a deep breath, and resumed his advance.

For who knew? Today might be his last day on Earth. If gravity kept buckling his knees, he wouldn't last till nightfall. He mustn't die without telling her of his deep affection for her.

He struggled back into the hallway and headed for the stairs. Harvey bounded alongside him, tongue out, nervous little growls coming out of him as his tail played along the bannister rungs, *platta-ta, platta-ta-plat.*

Mary had entered the bedroom, and was in the first stages of preparation for her much-loved afternoon shower. In this warm interlude, she slowly regrouped her forces in order to hold the world at bay for one more day.

At such a sacred hour, would she want an extra-terrestrial in the shower with her? Standing ankle-deep on duck feet and staring up at her with bulging and beseeching eyes?

It wasn't likely. But its probability was rapidly increasing, as E.T. mounted the stairs, once again humming, ". . . it's only rocks and rolling . . ."

Mary was spared this musical offering, as the faucets in the shower were now on. It took several minutes for the hot water to gyrate itself out of the boiler, and during these few moments she began to undress.

E.T. was just passing Mary's bedroom. He looked in and the plants keeled over, limp, possibly loaded, certainly confused. What was the ancient flower-master doing? The plants felt a vibration like the legendary swarms of bees from Venus, swarming from the ancient master's brain.

He continued down the hall toward the bathroom, vibrations of bee-sound preceding him, its point headed for the bathroom door.

Harvey cowered down, paws over his snout, as he was not allowed in the bathroom, ever since eating the bath mat. But the slamming bathroom door, the click of its lock, relieved the poor beast's anxiety.

E.T. stopped in the hallway outside it; the bee-squadron of Venus circled once, signaled with a brilliant light, and departed in a blur.

The elderly voyager shuffled back to his closet and fell onto the pillows, unconscious.

Keys did not know that he was already strangling his prize, that the array of elegant medical machinery in his warehouse had been sensed by E.T.'s telepathic beam, and that the signal filled the little being with heaviness. E.T. could not tell precisely what the signal meant, this varied pattern of light, this network of probes that kept assaulting his peripheral consciousness. But it had thrown him into melancholy, into depression, his body filling with a thousand vague anxieties, which his drinking bout did not dispel. Even as he lay in his closet, sprawled out, unable to lift his head, he could feel mechanical arms reaching out toward him, embracing him, holding him fast. He slept fitfully, with terrible visions troubling his dreams.

The source of these dark visions, a certain nearby warehouse, pulsed with its accelerating mission. Keys was exuberant, buoyed up by a vision of approaching triumph. His crew swirled around him in a kind of exultation; an important moment for Earth was approaching. Keys knew how important, for he had somehow touched the telepathic field of the civilization that had created and manned the Ship. Marvelous dreams had come to him, far outstripping anything of his childhood—and a strange love had grown in him, love for this beautiful intelligence that had flirted with Earth.

His team was in readiness, the countdown clicking. But all of this activity was somehow veiled by the continuous sensation he now had, of being with the Ship and its crew. Their power was a constant thought-wave flickering over him, monitoring him. He felt they would not find him wanting in compassion, or preparation. He had done everything he could to protect their stranded crewmate.

His fleet of vehicles gleamed, and where the doors were open, one could see the interiors gleaming too—readouts flashing, needles dancing, complex circuitry glowing.

He was bringing this to the lost creature from space, as an offering.

Elliott returned home, Lance the nerd at his side. "What happened to you in biology class, Elliott? You went crazy today, do you know that?"

"I know it."

"Bizarre behavior, Elliott. Don't you think it's uncool to draw attention to yourself—*at this time?*" The nerd gave Elliott a significant stare, like a mouse looking left and right after eating through a block of cheese.

Elliott stared back at him, and again resisted the impulse to kick Lance in the pants—for, as before, the nerd's squinty eyes were reflecting E.T.'s own eyes, tiny lights going off deep inside them.

Elliott sighed and walked toward the stairs, Lance following close behind him, like a persistent wad of gum on the sole of your shoe. "But I have to admit you gave it to that bio-creepo, Elliott. The kids from the class after ours said they came in and found him wiped out in his own ether. You know how ether-heads get, all out of synch, stumbling around? That's how he was . . ."

They entered Elliott's room, picked their way through the debris, and opened the closet, where they found E.T. on the pillows, toes in the air.

Lance was aghast. "You just leave him alone like this? Are you nuts? This is the most valuable thing in the world, anybody could break in here and kidnap him, or he could hurt himself or anything."

Elliott lifted the old voyager up from the pillow. "He's loaded."

E.T. opened his eyes. "Spell sixpack."

"You've had enough, E.T."

The ancient pilgrim from the stars made some cosmic finger signals, rotated his eyes, and hiccupped. Lance continued, appalled, "What do you want to hide him for, anyway? Do you know how many people pay good money to see KISS, for Pete's sake? He's bigger than KISS, he's bigger than the New York Yankees! Elliott, you have a gold mine here, Take him on the road."

Lance gestured, to show he had all the qualities it took to be a manager. His cowlick, glowing red, gave him the appearance of someone whose scalp had been elongated by a narrow escape from a cheese-loaded spring-trap; a big promoter would have had him thrown down the backstairs with the trash. But, being a nerd, he didn't know that. Nerdishly he pressed on. "You, me, and E.T. We'll make it legal."

Elliott kept E.T. upright, but the timeless traveler kept swaying back and forth. "Spell headache, Elliott."

"He's hung over," moaned Lance. "Elliott, you need a *handler* in here. You don't know the first thing about taking care of an extraterrestrial."

Elliott continued bracing E.T., but felt the heaviness in the old creature's body—a strange heaviness, a deep heaviness, unlike anything he'd ever handled.

"E.T." He shook the extraterrestrial, and E.T. turned his eyes upon him, but they held visions of the cosmos such as Elliott had never seen, not in all the weeks E.T. had been with him. They were the farthest-out signals imaginable. They hit Elliott all over the body, and the heaviness became his own.

"E.T., what's . . . happening . . ."

The ages-old being slumped forward. His density was changing. He was like the core of a collapsing star, the force of Earth's gravity fully upon him. He was becoming a black hole in space.

Lance was hit with it too, his own form weighted down, so that his lowness became still lower and he crouched, like a rat, under E.T.'s other arm. "Look, he communicates through you. He belongs to you. But you gotta make it legal. My dad's a lawyer. He'll figure something out. We'll be millionaires, we'll go everywhere. Everyone will want to know us because we'll be the most famous boys in the world. They'll all want to meet E.T. And he'll be *ours!*"

But E.T. wasn't anybody's, except gravity's. He had come fully to himself, had neutralized drunkenness out of his system with one instant's focus. But this other thing, this deep imploding of his being, that he could not change.

Ah, me...

He swayed back and forth, the contraction upon him. It was the end of his star-life. He was inwardly shrinking to the size of a pinhead. His span was over...

But he must not take the boy with him. And yet it was happening; the black hole was open and nothing could escape it. Those pilots who fly too close will be swallowed—that is the law of space.

"Spell...go away..."

He tried to move them back. But they were clinging to him, and he felt their love sweeping under each arm. Foolish children, you don't wish to follow me. For I am E.T. Your minds cannot follow where I go. I am an ancient traveler in the void, and you are puppies...

Harvey snuck into the room, head down, scowling. Mary was returning; the dog could feel her moving into range, and he must warn Elliott. He growled outside the closet door, and a moment later it opened.

He looked at the space creature, and his doggie mind saw a dark, cavernous force, into which light-bones were dropping, one after another. He jumped back, his own bones feeling the touch.

"Leave me..." said E.T., trying to lift his arms, but the Great Theory was working itself out in him, and his concentrated energy form, so perfectly suited for outer environments of space, was falling in on itself.

He had to find a way to die alone. But even then, the force might be so great that it would start to suck nearby forces into it. Could he, a single alien, implode the entire earth? Would his death turn it inside out?

"Spell...danger..."

He shifted through all the cosmic levels, but could not find a correct formula for neutralizing this. He was stuck fast, held, and his Ship was light-years away.

"He's...so heavy..." wheezed Lance, as they stumbled with him across the room. They lifted him up with all their might, and dumped him into Elliott's bed, just as Mary's footsteps reached the stairs.

A moment later she opened the door.

"Hi, guys..."

Harvey went up in front of her, begging with his paws. His hair stood out, incredibly magnetized, shielding Elliott and Lance as they whipped a blanket over E.T.

"What'd you do to Harvey?" asked Mary, as the dog panted in front of her, paws waving. "Did you drug him? Tell me the truth."

"Harvey," said Elliott, "cool it."

E.T. was dropping, dropping, deeper down. He

felt the willow-creature, mother of the house, and knew that she would be tugged in by his force—and he no longer wanted the intimacy, for he had a much different road from hers. Her cosmos and his were cross-related. She would never know where she was if she fell into his sinking depth. Her consciousness would disintegrate, as would that of the boys—

If I don't get up . . . get up . . . spell get up . . .

But he couldn't move; he could only listen, to the alien tongue of Earth.

"How was school?"

"Fine."

"Want something to eat?"

"We'll be down in a minute," said Elliott.

"Do you have . . . any Swiss cheese?" Lance was in need of a fix. His head seemed very weird all of a sudden. He felt himself dropping through something deeper than he'd ever dreamt of. It was like that night on his bike, but in reverse; then he felt he could almost fly, and now he felt caught in dark, sticky substances that only Swiss cheese could control.

"Somebody ate all the Swiss cheese already," said Mary, looking at the little nerd suspiciously. She knew something was up with these guys—it was tugging at her mother's intuition, but she didn't want to push it. And—she had a sudden, splitting headache. God, she hoped it wasn't early menopause. That was all she needed.

She walked out of the room. Elliott quickly turned back to E.T. The old wanderer's arm had fallen out from under the blanket. Horror crossed Elliott's face as he looked at the color of it—a grayish shade, which drew his gaze hypnotically into warps of dreaming he wasn't up to, at all.

He sank down, grabbing the old hand in his own. "E.T., heal yourself..."

Night had fallen. Elliott had brought in every medicine the family cupboard held, but they just lay in his room like toy medicines, useless for what ailed the creature lying in the bed.

E.T. was in the whirling vortex of the gravitational force. His dream of Earth-life, and his dream of starshine, was over. His sun was the black sun now.

And all because he couldn't resist...peeking in windows...

Somehow he must prevent his personal disaster from overtaking these Earthlings, or the Earth itself, for he didn't know—there was no formulated equation for this planet—it might indeed follow him if he went, for his body contained a great atomic secret.

Every plant in the house was dead. The walls themselves seemed to be heaving toward him, with each breath of his own lung.

"Heal yourself," begged Elliott again, for he felt that the old genius could do anything. But there are some things not even the elderly gods can accomplish.

E.T. slowly shook his head.

"Then give it to me," said Elliott, not knowing that in fact he already had too much of it, had the power to vanish into an alien world. But it was a power so old and so fast he could never control it, and the rush into the other dimension would scissor his consciousness in half.

"Carry me...far away..." whispered E.T. "...and leave me..."

"E.T.," said Elliott, "I'd never leave you."

The lost voyager summoned himself back toward the surface again, to speak, to plead. "I am...a grave danger to you..." He lifted the tip of his long finger. "...and to your planet..." He lifted his head, his star-eyes shining in the moonlight.

"But our communicator," said Elliott. "It's still working."

"Junk," said E.T.

His eyes flashed in the darkness. Within them, Elliott saw lines of incredible complexity stitching interstices of light, eyes comprehending collapsing depth-force. The ceiling groaned overhead. Harvey whined in the corner, and the unearthly eyes gazed on, at rushing mysteries of matter that no mere botanist of the stars could alter.

"You're not even trying," said Elliott, afraid of the eyes, and drawn to them. "Please, E.T."

The night passed on. E.T.'s body became more rigid, and gray all over. His lips moved, but no words came, only an inner rushing noise, of the ultimate compression of stellar matter. The mass of E.T.'s body, though no bigger than an umbrella stand, was of incredible density. His high energy load was being soaked up by his nucleus. Things were piling up inside him, squeezing his star-core.

Elliott's body felt as though it were made of chains, chains of iron holding him down. He felt heavier and heavier; his head was splitting, and dark depression weighed on him like a hundred thousand tons of lead. When the gray light of morning finally came, he pulled himself up and looked at E.T. The monster was like something drained, no longer gray, but white, a white dwarf.

Elliott dragged himself into the hallway, and staggered down it toward Mary's room. He pushed open the door, iron depression and cosmic loneliness all one to him now. He felt like an extraterrestrial, felt alien to himself, and he was afraid.

Mary opened her eyes, looked at him. "What's wrong?"

"Everything—is worth nothing," he said, feeling the deep in-falling, the collapsing, the departing.

"Oh, baby, that's no way to feel," said Mary, though in fact it was exactly how she felt too; all night she'd been dreaming she was underwater, unable to get to the surface.

"I have something wonderful," said Elliott, "and I've made it sad."

"Everyone feels like that now and then," said Mary, trying for an appropriate platitude, but it was no medicine for her, so why should it be any better for Elliott? She patted the bed, indicating the space beside her. Warmth was better than words, but her body felt cold in the gray dawn, chilled to the marrow, and chillier still as Elliott moved in beside her.

What was going on in the house? She sensed that there was something at its core, unnameable, horrible, gathering everything to it.

"Can you . . . tell me about it?" she asked.

"Later . . ." Elliott snuggled against her, but there was the same sense of falling, down, deeper into the vortex, where nobody's hands could reach them— because nobody existed.

"Go to sleep," said Mary, stroking his brow. "Go to sleep . . ."

Elliott slept, and dreamt of an iron ball, growing larger, then smaller, then smaller still, and he was riding it through nothingness.

When the seven-thirty alarm went off, Mary rose alone, leaving Elliott in his deep slumber. She knew he could fake fever, but this did not seem to be an act. As she put on her housecoat, a pull came into her eyelids, closing them. She pulled back, shook herself fully awake, and stared at Elliott. Yes, there was something not right about him today. Was he hung over? Was her baby following so fast in his no-good father's footsteps? She'd found six empty beer bottles . . .

The door opened, and Michael came in. "Where's Elliott?"

"Don't wake him," said Mary, and pushed Michael with her, into the hallway. "Do you know what's bothering him?" Mary tightened her housecoat. "He seems very depressed."

"Probably just school," said Michael. "School is depressing." The older brother glanced back down the hall. There was something wrong with E.T., there was something wrong with Elliott, and his own head was splitting.

"Well," said Mary, "I want him to rest."

"Let me stay with him," said Michael. "I only have a half-day of school today. Please, Mom . . ."

Mary took aspirin out of her housecoat. "All right," she said. "Maybe you can snap him out of it." She walked to the staircase, trying to shake her own stupor. Had she taken Valium by mistake last night? Her head felt like a lead balloon.

"Wake up now. Okay?" Michael sat on the bed beside Elliott. He lifted Elliott's eyelid, and the eye that stared back at him held no gaze he'd ever seen in his brother's eyes before—a gaze of stone.

Michael groaned and shook Elliott. "Please, Elliott, wake up..."

Elliott came around, slowly, and Michael helped him down the hall toward his room, the two brothers staggering against each other, Michael feeling like he was dragging an iron ball with him. What was this strange downward-tugging force? What had happened to his brother? What had happened to the house? Was it caving in or something?

Michael touched the wall to reassure himself, but the wall made other-dimension movements, its fibers charged with a subtle dance of dark light.

"Come on, Elliott, pull out of it..."

He dragged his brother into the bedroom; Elliott felt stiff, like chain, like iron.

And E.T. was stretched out under a blanket, turning as white as ash.

Michael dumped Elliott, fear rushing through him, a thousand dark dreams converging at a far-off center.

E.T. breathed in some deep ratio, off into his great atomic power. The god had to go. He was out of control.

Save me, he cried to his Captain, far in the night from here, sailing the Ship of Farthest Light.

Come, my Captain, come for the failing Botanist First Class.

My plants are dying.

And I too, I fear that I am dying.

"We've got to tell now, Elliott," said Michael. "We need help."

Elliott turned toward Michael, his eyes like moon jellyfish, swimming with danger, tentacles shining. "No, you can't, Mike. Don't..."

Elliott knew the rest of the world must not come in on them. The Army couldn't understand this. The government couldn't, either. They'd seize the miraculous creature and do things to him. "I'll split him half... with you," gasped Elliott. "That's as far as I'll go..."

Michael wiped his face, trying to think what half-power meant in the moral boundaries of their game. The power coming from the bed was rocking him back and forth on his heels, pushing him around the room like a puppet, and he knew it was more than they could handle, however the power was cut. It was beyond them by too much. The walls were radiating dark pulses, and Michael saw a thousand little shapes of E.T., with a cosmic fire burning behind him. Was the space creature going to burn the world?

"Elliott..." Michael staggered away, trying to shield himself from the wild dance of overcharged atoms. "We'll lose him if we don't get help. And Elliott, we'll lose you..."

Elliott's eyes were the red man-o'-war fish, reddish tentacles waving in his gaze. Power was there, beyond the Earth's perceiving. Elliott was glowing like iron in a furnace. He could always fake fever, but this...

Michael grabbed Elliott under one arm, and lifted E.T. with the other.

Mike was big, but the weight of these two creatures in his arms...

He strained with them, with Elliott's iron ball and E.T.'s cosmic sun. Michael's fingers twitched, E.T.'s forces moving them. E.T.'s touch was electric magic, and it was converging, ten million years' worth of spatial learning.

Flights to forgotten worlds of power, where he'd gathered much...

Michael dragged them into the bathroom and dumped them in the shower stall. He had to put out this fire, had to cool Elliott down...

The water came on, soaking Elliott and E.T.

The aged voyager shook his head as the water hit. Ah, yes, the shower, where the willow-creature dances.

E.T. felt Mary, felt the loveliness of her field, but he was moving into comet showers now. Goodbye, little willow...

He staggered forward, beneath the waterfall, but it was a waterfall on Venus, in a hidden grotto where secret rivers danced in darkness. E.T. closed his eyes and bathed there. All this, which he'd thought to visit everlastingly, would be gone.

He'd thrown it all away, curiosity killing the space cadet, as that well-known adage had it among fliers to strange worlds.

Peek in or out of the dimension, but don't get caught by death.

He'd thrown immortality away like the idiot he was. Though he'd clocked many star-miles, he'd slipped up.

And now, a last shower...

...which some take on Venus, some on Mars...

...but only a cosmic lunatic would get himself caught on Earth.

He splashed his duck feet, and sang softly, in a deep cosmic underground, through ancient reverberation chambers...

"...accidents will happennnnn..."

He sank down, knees made of lead, tons of it compressed there.

Elliott sank with him, dragged to the floor of the

tub. "E.T., heal yourself..." Elliott felt the power charges going off in him, but couldn't direct the force; it was just maniacal fire twitching in his limbs, and its healing ray was buried beneath waves of flame.

The door opened downstairs, and Mary came in, Gertie beside her.

"Go cheer up your brother," said Mary, sending Gertie along.

Mary set the groceries down, her splitting headache having returned the second she walked in the house. It felt like a knife blade, down the center of her forehead.

She moved her head back and forth, trying to see around it, then pressed her temples. She had a strong, sudden image of her doctor, prescribing things she didn't want...

Michael's thundering step of adolescence came down the stairs, each one of his footfalls like a ball of lead.

"Take it easy, honey," she said, "before you go through the floor."

"Mom, I have something to tell you. You'd better sit down..."

Mary sank back toward her chair. Oh, please, God, don't hit me with another childhood disaster, not today, not human bite marks on the chest or some other horrible boyhood fistfight story...

Her behind hit heavily, and she felt the chair creak, like tendons reaching the snapping point. "Is it something serious?"

"More serious than you can imagine."

She jumped up, head spinning, something terrible converging on her.

"Remember the goblin?"

Don't let it be a sex fiend, she said to herself. What had touched the family? Michael's eyes were like jellyfish.

Gertie's footsteps sounded on the stairs, and Mary felt the floor of the house shake—from the weight of a five-year-old child. "Mama," cried Gertie, "they're gone. They're not in the closet anymore!"

"They?" Mary looked at Michael.

"I'd better just show you," said Michael.

He led her up the stairs, to the bathroom. "Make the most excellent promise you can make..."

"Michael..." Mary's wits were falling out like hairpins, and Michael was talking like Dungeons & Dragons. "What *is* it?"

Michael pulled the shower curtain back. Mary blinked, her eyes remaining closed for one hesitant second, for she thought she'd seen a writhing coil of reptiles on the shower floor. As her eyes opened, she saw Elliott and—

"We're sick..." Elliott raised his hand. "...we're dying..."

The water was running over them, over Elliott and this monstrous shape, this tower of nightmares three feet tall. From the tower came a signal. The creature's lips were moving, and Mary heard split echoes, shattering cavernous spaces. "...will...ow...crea... ture..."

"He's from the moon," said Gertie.

Mary grabbed Elliott and dragged him from the

shower. She could think only of escape, from whatever it was that had held Elliott a moment ago, a wet reptilian thing, too monstrous to contemplate further. "Downstairs, all of you," she said, wrapping Elliott in a towel and pushing them all ahead of her. Her mind wasn't working rationally; she was running on some kind of twilight sense, groping blindly. The thing in the bathtub could stay there; she was getting out, with the kids. Beyond that, she had no other ideas or interests.

"We can't leave him alone," protested Elliott.

Mary just pushed forward. She had Absolute Power now, generated by overwhelming fear and the necessity for flight. She moved all three kids like rag dolls, toward the door. She opened it—and what last bit of reason she possessed failed her then, because there was an astronaut on the doorstep.

His eyes looked out through a domed helmet. His body was enclosed in a spacesuit. She slammed the door in his face and ran through the house to the side door. It was already opening, and another astronaut was entering.

Mary bolted for the window. A sheet of plastic came over it and she watched a man in a spacesuit taping it to the frame.

Then, moments later, an enormous plastic envelope came down, enclosing the entire house.

By nightfall the house had been converted into a gigantic, airtight package, draped in transparent vinyl, with huge air hoses climbing up over the roof and circling the structure. Bright lights, braced on tall scaffolding, illuminated it on all sides. The street was blocked off, and trailers and trucks were parked in the drive. Men came and went in blue jumpsuits.

Entry to the house was through a van.

Keys was in the van, just donning his jumpsuit and helmet. He opened the back door of the van and stepped into one of the enormous hoses. He walked along through it to a pneumatic seal; he unzipped it and entered the quarantined house.

" . . . astounding . . . simply astounding . . ."

The skeptical microbiologist was talking to himself inside his air helmet, his voice a strange wheezing, his face like a goldfish suffering shock in a dime-store bowl, as he stood dumbfounded in the area given over to his own team of specialists: men and women examining tissue slides and other samples from E.T.'s life-system, a system that had sent them all into momentary numbness, only some of which was wearing off now as they tried to cope with it.

In another area of the house, a team of doctors was working with members of the family. A sample of Mary's blood was being taken in a living room that had become an emergency ward.

"Have any environmental changes occurred since the . . . it . . . has been sequestered in the house? Temperature, humidity, light intensity?"

She stared at him, unable or unwilling to speak. Beside her, another doctor was taking Michael's blood pressure.

"Did you notice any superficial changes in the creature's skin color or in his breathing? Any hair loss, any evidence of surface sweating?"

"He never had any hair," said Michael.

"Apparently," one doctor said to another, "the children were able to establish a primitive language system with the creature. Seven, eight monosyllabic words."

"*I* taught him to talk," said Gertie to the doctor who was snipping a strand of her hair. A psychiatrist knelt before her.

"You taught him to talk?"

"With my Speak and Spell."

The psychiatrist had apparently never used one. "Have you seen your friend exhibit any emotions? Has he laughed or cried?"

"He cried," said Gertie. "He wanted to go home."

The leader of all this activity passed through, to the dining room, which was occupied by an X-ray team studying bone structures that had them scratching the sides of their helmets. Keys unzipped a plastic door and entered another room, where the quarantine had been most thoroughly imposed. The entire room was draped in plastic, and within it was still another room: a portable clean-room, ten feet by ten, plastic and transparent. Within it were Elliott and E.T., a team of medical specialists working around them.

"I'm getting a reading now, not a human EKG pattern."

"Any Q-, R-, X-waves?"

"No."

"Any waves at all?"

"I—I don't know."

The reading the specialist was getting had never been covered in any of the manuals. But doctors are funny fellows; give them a few minutes with any outrage of life, and they'll track it on their machinery, their calm somehow all-pervasive.

"That's odd..." was all one of them said, though it was exceedingly more than odd. Everything about the creature on the table before them was contradictory—parts of it like the quiet dreams of vegetables, and still other areas possessing the density of stone, low enough to paralyze the machines.

"Sonar, have you got a location on the creature's heart?"

"Difficult to see."

"Well, does it *have* a heart?"

"The entire screen is lit up. It looks like his whole chest is...a heart."

They poked him, prodded him, bent his limbs in all directions. Needles pricked his flesh in search of veins, other needles sought for reflexes. His ear-flaps were found, his delicate little ear-shoots opened. His universe-scanning eyes, supersensitive to light, were exposed to fierce, probing beams. The team worked feverishly, trying to unravel him from every possible angle at once, subjecting his tortured form to every possible scrutiny created by medicine to reveal the innermost workings of life.

The doctor who led the team kept trying to wipe his own brow, only to find it encased in glass. He was frustrated, confused, had begun to look upon E.T. as a creature dragged from the bottom of the sea, a monster of unconsciousness, an inhuman form whose meaning, purpose, and secret would ultimately evade him.

Awesome, yes, it was that, but its unspeakable ugliness robbed the doctor of his usual tenderness. His weary mind was seeing pterodactyls, primordial lizards, grotesqueries that should never have been and fortunately had ceased to be. This thing before him was one of them, cold and unfeeling, a creature out of one's nightmares—the deformed monster that one always feared would emerge from the womb of life. It was natural to hate such an object and wish it dead.

"It's alive," said the technician beside him, "but I can't find the breath..."

"...pulse remains steady..."

The elderly voyager lay still, like a dead moon. The bright fluorescent lights beat down upon him, a hideous human glare, shining deep into his nerves. He saw that he'd fallen under their spell, these Earth doctors who worked equipment of the crudest sort, compared to the delicate scanners on the Great Ship.

Ah, medicine, he sighed, calling to the Outer Night, where his own physicians were.

"Body looks like a marfans type."

"Write down *comparative exopthalmia*."

"Foot reflex reveals bilateral babinskis."

"...I'm getting a breath. Just one..."

He tried to feel his way toward the Ship, toward his higher purpose, for which he was much needed in the universe. Was he to lose all?

Ah, E.T., he sighed to himself, they have got you now.

The iron chains of Earth were on him. He was bound and shackled, and the weight was appalling, as his life-force continued its collapse.

"Have we got any type of trace elements?"

"We've established a radioactive threshold. But no evidence of superficial burning on the family, no bone damage."

"Doppler, have you picked up any blood flow?"

"I think we're seeing some blood in the inguinal area."

"We're picking up extra-systalyses—creature's reading and simultaneous boy's reading."

Again, the chief doctor nervously wiped his helmet. The boy and the monster were linked somehow, as if the monster were feeding on the child's life. The child came in and out of consciousness, hallucinating, babbling, sinking under again. I'd cut the cord that ties them, thought the doctor, if I only knew where and what it was.

He probed deeper, wiped his glass dome again. He was certain the creature was dying; his concern was now the boy. The heartbeat was irregular, the pulse weak, and all of it somehow synched with the monster, a hidden mesh that connected them in the most hellish way.

Goddammit, thought the doctor, with a glance toward the outer rooms, hasn't anyone figured this out yet?

He saw the domed nodding heads, nodding over their machinery, and he knew that nobody had any answers for this one.

He stared back down at the monstrous face. If ever there was an unfeeling, unrelated, cold, and loveless creature in the universe, it was this goddamn thing before him. Somehow it had evolved intelligence— for there'd been a spaceship—but the creatures who ran it were parasites, predators, incapable of sympathy, kindness, all the fine human things. He knew it as surely as he was standing here, and he wanted with all his heart to strangle the freak. It was dangerous; he could not say why, but his whole body knew it was dangerous to all of them.

A needle punctured E.T.'s skin. On the table beside him, Elliott winced, as if the puncture had been into his own body. He turned toward the only familiar face, toward Keys. "You're hurting him. You're killing us . . ."

Keys stared down at E.T. The vision he'd had of a noble space creature had altered radically in the face of E.T.'s ugliness; yet Keys' mind still burned with higher mental waves. This thing on the table before him, ugly as it was, was from the Ship, and the Ship was infinite in its sweep and power. To serve it was Keys' mission.

"We're trying to help him, Elliott. He needs attention."

"He wants to stay with me. He doesn't know you."

"Elliott, your friend is a rare and valuable creature. We want to know him. If we can get to know him, we can learn so many things about the universe and about life. You saved him and were good to him. Can't you let us do our part now?"

"He wants to be with me."

"He will be. Wherever he goes, you'll go. I promise you that."

But where the creature was going, none could follow. The whirling powers of his body were shifting at the core. The old being felt the enormity of this power, that of the ancient dragons. His race had harnessed this flame, this life. Was it to end in cataclysm? Was he to destroy this planet? No, he cried in himself, it must not come to that. What more horrible fate could there be than to destroy a thing so lovely as Earth? I would be cursed forever by the universe.

But the dragon at his center was dancing, eyes bright as burning suns, flaming with mysteries of terror and conquest. A potent force would be released, blowing doctors, machines, friend and foe, all, everyone, through the roof of space.

"The boy's unconscious again."

"Call in the mother."

E.T. clung at the edge of the void, on a last thin thread of energy. A roaring filled his ears, and the mouth of the dragon was open below him; awesome, black tongues of cosmic fire licked upward, eager to consume a planet, a solar system, whatever might come its way. E.T. felt the envelope of his nature rupturing and star-knowledge funneling out, faster and faster.

"I'm losing blood pressure."

"...and pulse..."

"Increase oxygen."

"This wave just went into V-Tak!"

"V-Tak or artifac? How can you tell with no Q, R, or X?"

"He just went straight-line duc."

"Zap him!"

An electrical device was applied to E.T.'s chest. They zapped him, injected adrenalin, pounded on him.

"Nothing...I'm drawing a blank here..."

The old space voyager's EKG reading was a solid, steady line, heart action ceased. E.T. lay dead—but Elliott stirred, all of his strength returning almost at the moment the old voyager's heart had ceased. E.T. had found at least one of the formulas he sought, that of a shield, cast behind him as he swooned into death, so the boy could not follow.

Elliott jerked upright in bed, screaming, "E.T., don't go!"

"No response," said a doctor. "No breath."

"He can *hold* his breath," cried Elliott.

The doctors shook their heads. The creature they'd tried to save was gone, and now their outraged sensibilities began to reel once more; what had it been they were working on?

They hardly noticed the momentary flicker in the lights, and in the equipment, nor did they fully perceive the trembling of the house, the valley. This was reserved for other men, other equipment, those that monitor disturbances deep in the Earth's core...

Keys, like a child who cannot believe that death really exists, leaned in beside the extraterrestrial, and whispered, "How do we contact your people?"

Elliott didn't feel Mary's hand on his shoulder, felt nothing but his loss. "He was—the best," sobbed Elliott, eyes swimming with sorrow as he gazed at his ancient friend. Behind him, Gertie and Michael entered, over the protests of the chief doctor.

Gertie went over to the table and stood on tiptoe, looking at the monster. "Is he dead, Mommy?"

"Yes, honey."

"Can we wish for him to come back?"

The last thing in life Mary would wish for was the little monster to come back. She gazed at his hideous shrunken form, his horrible mouth, his long creepy fingers and toes, his grotesque stomach—it was all ugliness, and it had nearly killed Elliott.

"I wish," said Gertie. "I wish, I wish, I wish..."

I wish, thought Mary, repeating the child's verse, for reasons she couldn't sort out.

The clean-room was cleared of everyone, including Elliott, who stood outside it now, staring in as E.T. was zipped into a plastic bag and covered with dry ice. Behind him, the other rooms were being stripped of their machinery and their protective vinyl coatings.

A small lead coffin was brought, and taken into the clean-room. Agents placed the extraterrestrial in the box.

Keys came behind Elliott and put his hand on the boy's shoulder.

"Would you like to see him one last time?" Keys

waved the other agents out and sent Elliott in alone, the plastic flap dropping closed behind him.

Elliott stood over the little coffin. He brushed the dry ice away from E.T.'s face. The tears in Elliott's eyes spilled down his cheeks and fell onto the plastic film covering E.T.'s wrinkled brow. "I thought I'd get to keep you forever. And I had a million things to show you, E.T. You were like a wish come true. But it wasn't a wish I knew I had, till you came to me. Have you gone some place else now?"

Do you believe in fairies?

Geeple geeeple snnnnnnnnnnnnn org

A beam of golden light shot through inner space. Historians of the cosmos are divided as to the direction from which it came. It was more ancient than E.T., older than the oldest fossil. There are those who claim it was the healing soul of Earth itself, flickering a single thread of what it knew, as a gesture of diplomacy perhaps, toward its alien visitor.

"Don't peek in any more windows," some say it said, and was gone.

Others say the Earth was doomed and could not save itself, that the saving force had come from a sister planet, to lend a hand in pacifying the dragon of the nuclear force.

And still others heard: *dreeeple zoonnnnnnnggggggg ummmmmtwrrrdssss*

Calling from the beyond.

Whatever it was, it touched E.T.'s healing finger, and caused it to glow.

He healed himself.

He did not know how.

But he had a vision of his Captain, more beautiful than any could imagine.

Good evening, Captain, said E.T.

Don't peek in windows, said the answering voice.

Never again, my Captain.

A brilliant glow filled E.T.'s entire body, and he felt golden all over, but especially in his heart-light, where the gold transmuted to red, on and off. The steam, rising from the dry ice, turned pinkish, tinted with color. Elliott noticed it, scraped away the ice from E.T.'s chest, and saw the glow of the old voyager's heart-light.

He turned toward the door, where Keys was still talking to Mary. He quickly covered E.T.'s heart-light with his hands.

E.T.'s eyes opened. "E.T. phone home."

"Okay," said Elliott in a joyful whisper. *"Okay."* He removed his shirt and laid it over the heart-light. "We've got to sneak you out of here. Stay put..."

Elliott laid the dry ice back in over E.T., and zipped the bag closed. Then, feigning grief, he went out through the flap, face in his hands, pushing past Mary and Keys. In another second he was in the kitchen alongside Michael and a table cluttered with surgical tools, face masks, and microscopes. On the table was E.T.'s wilted geranium. As Elliott whispered to Michael, the geranium, like Michael, lifted its head, and a moment later, fresh green leaves shot out of its dead stems. Buds appeared. It bloomed again.

Michael made one quiet phone call and then slipped out the side door.

Elliott was standing at the main air tube leading from the house as the agents came by, carrying the lead box. They opened the zipper door, the key-man holding it for them. They carried the coffin through the hose, deposited it in the van, and returned.

"I'm going with E.T.," said Elliott.

"You and your family will go with me, Elliott. We're all going to the same place."

"Where he goes, I go. You promised. I'm going with him now."

Keys sighed, pulled the zipper door back, and let Elliott through. Elliott scrambled up into the van, and knocked on the door to the cab. Michael, in the driver's seat, turned. "Elliott, there's just one thing. I've never driven forward before."

Then he put the van in gear, stepped on the gas, and pulled away. A horrible ripping sound signaled that the entire hose system was tearing from the house, and as it tore away, the enormous plastic envelope surrounding the house collapsed. The van skidded to the bottom of the drive, trailing twenty feet of main hose behind it like the flailing tail of a dragon.

Michael leaned on the horn. Policemen scurried to move the crowd barriers and the crowd parted to let the van through. Elliott bounced around in back as the van slid into the open. Only then did he notice that two agents were inside the hose that trailed the van, the agents clinging to the hose's ribs and trying to climb forward.

And had he been able to look out the other end of the hose, he would have seen Mary jumping into her car with Gertie.

She was pulling down the drive, past government vehicles, in pursuit of the van and hoping that the theft of it, just perpetrated by her children, wasn't actually a criminal act, though she strongly suspected it was.

"Where are we going, Mommy?" asked Gertie.

"For placenta cream," said Mary, screeching through the opening in the police barricades.

"Did Elliott and Michael steal the van?"

"Yes, dear . . ."

"Why didn't they take *me* with them?"

"Because you're too young to be stealing vans," said Mary, barreling down the street. "When you're older, then you can."

She squealed around the corner, after the wayward van. She knew now that the monster was alive, knew it in every tortured nerve-ending of her body. And whether wishes or just dumb luck had brought it back to life, she was glad, for though it was causing still further complications in her situation—though police cars were now chasing her, and it, she knew that somehow—it was the best.

• • •

The bouncing agents struggled up the hose, clinging to its swaying shape. At the mouth of it they could see Elliott, working frantically.

Hey, thought one of them, that kid isn't trying to unlatch this hose, is he?

A moment later the agent was rolling in the street, hose collapsed around him and his colleagues, as the van sped on, leaving them behind.

Michael fought the wheel and pedals of the zooming van. "We're gonna get killed, Elliott," he called over his shoulder. "And they're never gonna give me my license."

He marveled at the way other cars moved aside just before the moment of collision; and the van whipped on. Elliott climbed up to E.T.'s bouncing lead box, opened it, and unzipped the plastic bag.

E.T. sat up, brushed the dry ice off himself, and looked around. "E.T. phone home."

"Are they coming for you?" asked Elliott.

Zeeeep zeeple zwak-zwak

E.T.'s eyes were bright, but even brighter was his heart-light, which answered Elliott with a brilliance that filled the van.

Michael whipped the van off the avenue and onto the road that climbed a hill called the Lookout. And looking out from the Lookout were the Dungeons & Dragoners he'd phoned a half hour earlier. They were waiting now, with bicycles.

The van streaked to a stop, and Elliott and Michael helped E.T. down.

The Dungeoners—Greg, Tyler, and Steve—stood openmouthed as the little monster was brought toward them.

"He's a man from outer space," said Elliott, "and we're taking him to his ship."

As the doctors' minds had reeled earlier, so now the Dungeoners reeled. But in the Game they'd played all parts—mercenaries, orks, wizards, knights—and somehow it prepared them for the amazing. So, though their minds had just fallen apart, they nevertheless helped E.T. into Elliott's bicycle basket and then raced off, down one of the four roads that ran up to the Lookout.

Tyler led, long legs pumping up and down on his pedals. A glance back over his shoulder gave him another mind-boggling view of the thing in Elliott's basket, and he pumped faster, eager to get rid of it in a hurry, whatever it was. Before it started multiplying.

"Elliott!" screamed Greg, spit flying behind him. "What . . . what . . ." But his tongue fumbled in his moist mouthful, and he could only dribble in wonder as he pumped for all he was worth. Beside him, Steve was hunched over his own handlebars, winged hat on, wings bent by the wind. He too glanced at the monster and knew that whatever it was, it was somehow related to letting your kid sister make you bake mud pies. He'd fill in the details later. But a deep vow was born in him at that moment, never ever to have anything to do with anybody's sister anymore, including his own. Weird things could happen, such as he'd probably learn about in freshman hygiene class. He bent further over the handlebars, his young mind raging with unanswered questions, his feet flying on the pedals.

As this strange crew of cyclists dipped out of sight, the hilltop filled again, with government vehicles, police cars, and Mary. They all screeched to a stop around the van and the police leapt out, guns drawn. Mary leapt out at the same moment, and ran toward the police, screaming, "No, they're only children!" Months of frustration, fear, and plain craziness filled her voice; the police drew back, startled, as she pushed past them. If she'd been this convincing in divorce court, she'd be a richer woman today.

The momentary diversion increased the bikers' distance from the police, who were still dealing with the van and the dry ice that was spilling out of it. But when the doors were fully opened, it was seen to be empty.

At that moment, from the bushes emerged another figure who'd somehow known that this place was the most important spot in the world this evening. "They took their bikes!" screamed Lance. "I know where they're going!"

Mary clamped her hand over the little nerd's mouthful of buckteeth, and dragged him into her car. But Lance rolled down the window and shouted to the police and government agents. "The lake, they're headed for the far side of the lake!"

The police sailed off with the agents, in the direction of the lake.

Lance turned to Mary. "The forest—I'll show you."

"But—the lake?"

"Hey, I may be a nerd, but I'm not stupid, you know."

E.T. and company pedaled on along the winding pavement, toward the landing site. The Dungeoners kept looking at E.T., their minds disordered from the sight of him, but their hearts telling them another thing, wordless and forceful: that he was their friend and this was the Game at last, in its highest form. They pedaled harder, faster, bearing him off to whatever awaited him.

The police cars were circling the lake, past camps, cottages, the park attendant's shack. "Naw, nobody's been here..." The attendant stared at the vehicles piling up on the dirt road. "What's goin' on?"

Wheels spun, tires sent mud and stones shooting in the attendant's direction, and then the chase team was gone, back along the lake road to the pavement again.

Which way? wondered the lead driver, a police sergeant with one twitching eyelid, twitching all morning, as though something were signaling inside it. It twitched his wheel to the left and he was moving, following some inner radar.

The cars behind followed him, racing back along the highway, accelerators down, government agents insisting on fancy floorwork; this chase was big, and nothing could get in its way. "Fork here—spread your men out—"

Radios signaled across the chase, and the cops branched out, forming a fan whose support lines were the grid of streets, a fan that kept wheeling and turning, opening and closing, one block after another.

"...turn, turn..." The twitching eyelid twitched and car wheels twitched with it, closing in again on some weird signal up ahead, a signal reaching all of the drivers from the heart of their quarry, an extraterrestrial whose excited communication band was searching the heavens with a telepathic probe so strong that even the stones could feel it.

E.T. bounced in Elliott's basket, hanging on to it with his long fingers. His head was buzzing with signals, buzzing with

znackle nerk nerk snackle do you read us?

Yes, my Captain. But please hurry will you *zinggg zingle nerk nerk*

Tyler's long legs were blurred pedalwork, knees pumping his ten-speed, leading the crowd, Michael beside him, hunched over his own set of wheels. Faintly, Michael heard the siren.

"They're coming!" He shot a glance toward Elliott.

"The alleyway!" shouted Elliott, cutting in ahead of both of them, Greg and Steve following, spit flying, wings folded back. Slim rubber tires screeched as they skimmed into the alley's broken asphalt; the alley was the trunk line to their destination, to the far hills, which felt farther off than they ever had before.

The bikes bounced and swerved over the cracks,

and the backs of the houses glanced, windows blinking, shaded eyelids going up. A hand, holding a can of beer, brought the can to lips that trembled for a moment, blinds pulled aside. Did I just see a monster go by in a basket?

A belch followed, another, and then a heavy footstep toward the old liquor cabinet. A man needs a chaser after a sight like that. I've got to cut back on this stuff...

"Hang a right..." The agent pointed, his fingertip seeming to glow. How do I know where to go? he asked himself. I just know that I know. Up there... there...

Car wheels spun toward the alley. Police cars hit it in seven different places, then formed a caravan over the broken pave. The lead car, still wheeled by the twitching-eyed sergeant, shot through the narrow corridor, siren going, the sergeant's good eye working double-time, but God help the little old lady, he thought, who steps out from behind the garbage cans for a smoke. Because we'll drive her right over the goddamned clothesline into next week.

On the outer edge of the fan, the agents were closing, cutting off the far end of the alleyway. A glowing finger pointed, glowing with absolute certainty.

"There they are!"

Elliott spun his wheels, jumped off his bike, and ran it up a flight of concrete steps, beside an old garage. Michael and Tyler were right behind him, bouncing up with him, into a backyard, shielded by wooden fences on both sides.

Greg foamed over the top step, Steve beside him, wings up as they stopped, took their bearings, and then shot out into the next alleyway.

Tyler was already there, sliding right, Michael sliding with him, and Elliott and E.T. between them. E.T. stared around, enormous eyes revolving. *Don't let me be caught xyerxyer nark vmmmmmmmnnnn* can you hear me?

zerk, nergle vmmmmnnnn znack our great Captain bids you hurry, danger danger danger

The alleyway bent in a gentle upward arc, skimmed by five bicycles bearing one monster toward the high hills, through the back way, the inner circuit known better to bikers than to car-jockeys. The big vehicles came against each other, one line lower, were blocked, had to back off, turn, start again.

"Slippery little rats," said the sergeant leading, his left eye fluttering like a strobe light, faster than eyelids are supposed to go. He backed over some ashcans, hoped there was no old lady, dog, kid, or sacked-out drunk behind or inside them, because they were under his wheels if they were. He accelerated forward, siren wailing, cap visor tugged down over the bridge of his nose in determination. He roared out the far end of the alley and turned left again, following his eye.

"The little bastard . . ." Agent Keys was mumbling to himself. "The no-good little sonofabitch." Elliott's sweet, lying face was with him. The kid will go far in life with a face like that. Screw you all up, just at the last moment, when you have the trophy in your hand.

"Turn, turn!" he screamed, knowing the course, feeling it in his fingers, his toes. His driver wheeled it, setting a new pattern, back out into the street, just as Tyler and Elliott appeared from the alley.

"Shit," said Tyler, "there they are..."

The last piece of street in their path, the last city block before the forest, before escape, was suddenly filled, agents on both ends, cops in the middle, as doors opened and personnel spilled out.

Elliott wheeled back around toward the alley. The snout of a police car appeared there, pursuit lights whirling, the car bearing down.

The fan had closed all the way now, tight in to the center, folding in completely on the boys. Tall Tyler crouched over his ten-speed. "Let's just try and crash them." He pedaled forward, Michael beside him, and Elliott right behind, bikes revved as fast as they could go. There was some space, a narrow channel between two of the parked vehicles. Tyler pointed, Elliott nodded. Greg and Steve flanked the flying wedge, Greg's mouth finally dry, parched, spitless for the first time in years. "We can't make it," he said, but he bent over his handlebars, wishing he had just one bubble left to blow in their faces. Steve's wings bent flat against his head, pressed by the driving wind of his speeding bike. If he angled it right, he could plow right into a cop and spend the night in jail.

The phalanx of bikes drove toward the wall of police, government agents, paramilitaries. All the corridors were blocked.

One last crash, thought Elliott. That's all we could give him.

E.T. raised a finger and gave a little lift to the chase. The bikes shot into the air, over the tops of the pursuit cars.

"I'll be goddamned," said the chief of police, hands on his hips, cap tipped back, gaping.

Five bicycles were sailing over the houses.

Keys felt his stomach falling toward his feet, as if he'd just walked off a building. The bicycles skimmed the telephone wires, then the tops of the poles, and then disappeared into the twilight, leaving nothing behind but a winged hat.

E.T. gazed down at the ground below. Yes, this was much better, a smoother ride. His heart-light had come on again, and was shining through Elliott's bicycle basket into the dusk.

An owl, lately returned to his favorite tree, woke up and shifted his wings, lazily. Time to bite the old mouse . . .

He lifted himself aloft.

What in heaven's name . . .

Five flying bikes sailed by the bird, who rolled over backwards in the air, beak snapping nervously. E.T.'s heart-light caught his powerful gaze. He stared at the elderly goblin, whose own eyes were slitted in third awareness, watching the night.

The bats are getting bigger around here, thought the owl.

Or I've lost my mind.

The bikes were already gone, into the falling darkness. Elliott angled his, in the pattern he knew now, and the others followed, gliding in his path.

"Tell me when it's over," drooled Greg, eyes closed, wet lip drooping. Beside him Steve's hatless head was flying hair, raised to the tip-ends as he stared at the ground below. Sisters, he said to himself softly.

Tyler and Michael were flanking Elliott, and E.T. was gazing into the distant sky, his outer awareness probing beyond the clouds.

znack zerkle dergggg oh, my Captain, is it really you?

znerkle derggg dergggg

A telepathic face appeared to him, that face most trusted, most perfect and sublime of all the ancient travelers. It smiled its turtlish smile of highest consciousness, and then was gone, into hidden bands of rushing descent.

"The forest!" shouted Elliott, as the bikes banked in the sky, and the others could see it ahead—the rolling hills and then the deep shadows.

Mary, grounded, but moving along, maneuvered her car up the same hillside, instructed by her nerd. "On up the fire road," said Lance, morosely. The greatest bike chase of all time and he wasn't in it. Why?

Because he was . . .

A nerd.

Gertie sat between them, the geranium in her lap. More new blossoms were opening in it, petals unfolding as Mary bounced the car up the fire road.

Lance gazed ahead at the dark treetops. "I'm getting some heavy signals," he said. "Park here..."

They parked, got out, and entered the woods, Lance leading, Mary holding Gertie's hand. Their path was slow, but the path above treetops is not, and Elliott led his party along it, swiftly, to the hidden communicator.

"There..." E.T. pointed with his finger, and the flying bicycles went into a descent pattern. They glided lightly down, touched in the grass, and rolled to a stop.

Ulllll-leeple-leep

The communicator hummed. As Elliott approached it, a sudden beam of brilliant lavender light broke over him. He froze in it, looked at E.T. The old monster stepped into the light with him, and together they looked up.

The Great Ship was overhead, soft lights glowing. It seemed to Elliott as if an enormous Christmas tree ornament had fallen from the darkness. He stared at the beautiful vehicle, drinking in the greatness of its power. It was E.T. multiplied a millionfold, the greatest heart-light the world had ever seen. Its mysteries shone into him, and messages of love and wonder ran up and down his body, melting him to nothing. He turned toward E.T.

The ancient voyager's eyes had grown bigger too, filling with the sight of the beloved mother Ship, Queen of the Milky Way. Her command lights shone their elegant patterns around her hull, and he felt the mind of the cosmos therein, in its most evolved form.

He looked at his friend, who had helped him to call across an incalculable distance. "Thank you, Elliott . . ." His voice had become stronger, as its overtones increased in harmony with the Ship, defining higher and higher patterns of energy.

I promise, he said to the glowing hatchway, not to peek in windows.

But at that moment he felt another pattern entering the clearing, and there was the willow-creature, and he gazed at her in silence for a long moment.

Gertie ran toward him. "Here's your flower," she said, holding out the geranium.

He lifted her into his arms. "B. good."

A shadow moved at the edge of the clearing, and the sound of jingling keys filled the night. E.T. quickly set Gertie down. He turned to Elliott, and held out his hand. "Come?"

"Stay," said Elliott.

The old voyager embraced the boy, and felt the cosmic loneliness run through him, as deep as any he'd ever felt. He touched Elliott's forehead, and made the intricate wave-sign over it with his fingertips, to release the child from the narcosis of the stars. "I'll be right here," he said, fingertip glowing over Elliott's chest.

Then the old botanist walked up the gangplank. The inner light of the Great Gem glowed above him, and he felt the millionfold circuits of its awareness lighting in him, until his heart, like Elliott's, had filled, not with loneliness but with love.

He went into the misty light, with his geranium.